The Road Home: Frank's Story

Timothy D. Alexander

Copyright © 2023 by Timothy D. Alexander

The Road Home: Frank's Story

by Timothy D. Alexander

Printed in the United States of America

ISBN 979-8-9883802-0-7

Life's Journey

Zachary, La.

(225) 522-1266

shalom2u@bellsouth.net

Contents

Dedication

This book is dedicated to my lovely bride, Mary. Thank you for being my biggest fan.
To my children, Lia and Andrew: Remember, God has a plan and a purpose for your lives.
To my parents, Larry and Nora Beth, for raising us in a Christian home full of love.
To my friends and family, thank you for your support.

Introduction

As we travel on life's journey, sometimes the road is smooth, and sometimes it is full of obstacles and potholes. We sometimes make wrong turns and end up on the wrong path. The hope of the author is that the journey of a teenage boy named Frank "Tank" Carter, and the people he encounters along the way, will entertain the reader. The desire is for the reader to make a connection with at least one character. If you find yourself on the wrong path, the *Way* is a prayer away.

Chapter One
Time to Blow, Then Go

"I don't need a lecture!" Frank argued as he tried to brush past his dad.

"All I'm saying, son, is as long as you live under my roof, you live under my rules." Joe half stepped to his right to block his son on the top step of the porch.

"Chill out, Dad! My friends and I were out celebrating, you know, blowing off a little steam. You gotta understand, we just finished finals and stuff, so the guys and I needed a little party to help us relax." It felt much warmer and dryer than the 74 degrees reading on the porch thermometer.

"Son, you have been celebrating and blowing off steam since football season ended." Joe felt his throat tighten, and his mouth went dry; he did not want this conversation, but it had to happen. "Last weekend's celebration almost landed you in jail. Frank, son, this coming home all hours of the morning, smelling like a barroom, has got to come to a stop—now."

Joe had heard Frank rumbling up the drive and was out the door before the swirling dust kicked up by the Harley could settle. He met his son on the front porch before he could make it into the house and retreat to his bedroom. Joe had let more than a few things slide in recent weeks, but this was the final straw. Last weekend, the police brought Frank home after they found him slumped over the handlebars of his Harley in a drunken stupor on the side of the road.

Sue could not stand to hear them argue, but there was no way she was getting involved in this one. She knew it was best to let them yell it out. They were more alike than either one of them would ever admit. They would blow up, yell, scream, holler, then go to a neutral corner and cool off. Everything would be all right in a little while, she prayed.

"I'll be outta here. . . . gone . . . hours away at college in less than three months. Then what are you going to do, Dad? Maybe you and Mom should pack up and go with me! Huh? Is that what you want?"

Frank felt like his head was going to explode. The combination of too much alcohol and other unseen dark forces crowded in his mind had Frank's head pounding. Suddenly, he felt like walls were closing in around him as Rage and Anxiety tightened their grip. Pressure had been building for months, similar to the rumblings of Mt. St. Helens; now was the time for a huge eruption.

"I'm eighteen years old, almost nineteen. I am a man, and I don't need a mother-efffff, um mom, following me around, babysitting me." Frank came dangerously close to dropping the f-bomb and a whole stream of vile words that were bouncing around in his head. Luckily, his brain, now in a semi-sober state, had managed to divert them before his tongue could utter such profanity.

Sue cringed, winced, and bit her bottom lip as she stood inside the front door and whispered, "Thank you, Jesus, he did not let that word slip." She was also glad they lived outside of town and a mile from the nearest neighbor.

Joe clenched his fist and teeth, and with temples throbbing, he stepped forward, looking up only slightly to his six-foot-four inch, two-hundred-forty-pound, all-state linebacker son, preparing to put him over his knee somehow and whip his butt. Joe had spent his childhood in a house with an alcoholic, abusive, foul-mouthed dad, and he did not use, nor did he tolerate, cursing in his home. Wisdom, respect, or maybe even fear, whatever it was, Frank had no desire to physically challenge his dad, who stood only half an inch shorter but equally as broad in the shoulder as he. Frank knew his dad was *farm boy strong* and could tell by the look on his father's face he was serious, and this conversation was going to happen right then and there.

"I know I've said this a thousand times: if you live under my roof, you live under my rules!" Joe hissed through clenched teeth and stepped even closer, close enough for his son to smell the coffee on his breath.

Frank popped back his tongue like a striking cobra before he could catch himself, "I'm tired of living under your rules, and I'm tired of living under your roof. I'm out of here!"

Frank brushed past Joe, who stood firmly planted just off the bottom step. He stormed up the front steps, across the porch, and grabbed the screen door, almost ripping it off the hinges.

"You better stop and think about it, son!" Joe responded with the first words to pop in his head.

Bam!

The front door, which Joe had left slightly ajar, flew open and hit the wall and rattled every picture Sue had hanging in the living room. She stood speechless, mouth opened wide, with tears in her eyes; thankfully, she had stepped back when she heard Frank stomp across the porch. Things had gotten way out of hand in a hurry. She tried to step toward her baby boy to make it better but froze in her tracks as Frank glared her way and muttered, "I have thought about it; Dad, that's why I'm outta here!"

Sue realized by the rage in his eyes and growl in his voice this was not her baby boy; a wave of chills shuttered her entire body. He had glared straight at her but was so blind by rage he had not even seen her. She did not see the sky-blue eyes of a loving son but bloodshot eyes filled with anger and a face distorted by hate and rage; it was evil. Sue felt dizzy; she felt her face go pale as the blood rushed away, and fear tried to take over her emotions. Stepping back half a step, she grabbed the back of the couch and steadied herself.

"Help, Lord!" The words formed on her trembling lips but with no sound. "I need you, Lord," Sue gasped for breath as Fear tightened his grip.

"Not today!" said Peace as his backhanded blow drove Fear far from Sue. A supernatural peace flooded over Sue, reassuring her God was in control.

Blam, blam, blam, blam. Frank stormed upstairs, hitting every third step. His mind was racing, bombarded with thousands of thoughts, some of them his own; some placed there by an unseen enemy lurking about, seeking only to devour. *I've got to get out of this house. I can't take it anymore!*

Frank went through a mental checklist. "Grab the duffel-bag. Shove in the bedroll, jeans, t-shirts, sweatshirt, and denim jacket. If he tries to stop us, I swear . . ." Anger rose and wrapped his leathery wings around the head of his latest toy. The stench of burning sulfur in the unseen realm of the fourth dimension overwhelmed the room, serving as a reminder to any warriors of the Holy One that they could not interfere. This unholy one, known as Anger, had been granted legal access and did not plan to relinquish his newfound home. With supernatural surgical precision, Anger dug his razor-sharp talons deeper into Frank's skull, straight to the cerebral cortex; Anger had mastered the ability to control thoughts and responses through lies and manipulation.

"I will show the old man I am not a kid anymore!"

Frank's mind was racing. This was it. Pride wouldn't let him turn back. "Hurry, gotta go. Now . . . now . . . think . . . think . . . Come on, Frank, what else? Money . . . top-drawer . . . at least a thousand in graduation money."

Frank grabbed his hunting knife because you never know what might happen on the road. His heart was racing and his head pounding—the stress, the rules—gotta go, gotta get on the Harley and get the hell out of here. The spirits that had taken up residence in

Frank's inner man to torment him were driving him, pushing him, compelling him to leave. His mind had become a spiritual battleground for the things of God ingrained in him from as far back as he could remember versus the things of the world. Right now, the things of the world were winning as dark unseen forces darted around his mind and attempted to extinguish any glimmer of hope or light. His dad represented what Frank considered an old-fashioned, dead religion that he neither needed, wanted, nor had any room for in his life. Right now, everything in him despised everything his father represented.

"If I don't get out of this house right now . . ." Frank gritted his teeth and snarled in a most unholy tone from deep within, a sound that surprised him for a split second. The spirit of destruction knew, from many millennia of practice, the best plan of attack was to get Frank out from under Joe and Sue's roof—more importantly, out from under their spiritual covering.

Clomp! Clomp! Clomp! Clomp! Frank barreled downstairs toward the front door. There was Mom; tears streamed down her cheeks as she stood between the stairs and the front door.

"Crap, almost made it," Frank muttered under his breath. He felt a twinge, a spark of hope deep inside like a lost little boy crying out for his mom. Sue noticed his eyes soften for a split second then harden again as Anger and Resentment quickly ran across the battlefield of Frank's mind and crushed the memory of that little boy and his happy childhood. Compassion had almost created a crack in the wall these unholy warriors had worked so feverishly to create.

"Don't try and stop me, Mom!"

"Where are you headed, Tankie?"

"I don't know, Mom, all I know is . . . is . . . I've got to get out from under *his* rules and *his* roof!" Frank cut his eyes toward the front porch where he had left Joe. "I am eighteen. I am a man! I am tired of being treated like a kid!"

Sue softly whispered, "I know you are grown, but no matter how old you are, you will always be my little Frankie Tankie."

Frank rolled his eyes as the spirits desperately tried to tear away at the bond he had formed over the last eighteen years with his mom. Mom had called him Frankie Tankie ever since Coach Harold Tucker called him Frank the Tank in pee-wee football. Everybody else called him Tank, but for Mom, it was Frankie Tankie. She was the only one that could get away with it. The tormenting spirits knew that bond would not be broken easily, so their plan of attack was simple: time to run away.

"Mom . . ."

Not pulling any punches, Deception threw a jab, whispering in Frank's spiritual ear. "She is on hisssss side; she doesn't want to let you grow up. It is time to be a man!"

Swooping in and out of Frank's mind, the demon taunted, "If you don't leave now, you will never be able to leave."

The dark visitors from the fourth dimension were almost dragging him out the door physically. Demons knew to gain victory, they had to get Frank away from praying parents and the members of the army of light encamped around the home—right now. Knowing they had legal access to the human but not to this home, it was time to go.

Chapter Two
Hit the Road; Don't Look Back

N *o time for this sentimental bull——.*
Frank's head felt like it is going to explode as the evil influences tightened an unseen vice on his head. *Move quick. . . . out the front door . . . across the porch . . . down the steps . . . there's Dad, looking busy with yard work!*

The voices in Frank's head urged him on, "Be a man! No more of this kid stuff! Don't look Dad's way or say a word; he might try to stop us. . . . just gotta get away!"

Even though Frank did not look, the unholy warriors glared in Joe's direction, swords were drawn, ready for a fight. Very much aware of the presence of a multitude of Heavenly Warriors swarming the front yard, swords also drawn, the dark ones huddled around their latest host just in case there was a last-second attack. Swords that gleamed from the Son's light were also on high alert in case one of the dark ones made a move. Angels of Light knew they could not interfere where the dark ones had been given legal access, but they were fully prepared to shield the ones belonging to the Lamb.

Frank mumbled to himself as he strapped the duffle bag to the sissy bar. "Make sure it's tight. Wouldn't want all my earthly possessions blown all over the highway." Frank laughed to himself, *Did I pack clean underwear?* Mom's voice rang in his head, "Frankie, did you remember to pack clean underwear?" Enough of the emotional bull-crap; the dark forces drove the wedge deeper to reinforce the walls of resentment in the inner recesses of his head.

Demons frantically attempted to block any emotional responses that may have drawn him back inside and, most importantly, back to the right path. "It's time to go. . . . get on the highway and ride like the wind." He tugged on his helmet, turned the key, and gave the V-twin a good swift kick. *Blap! Blap! Blap!* No mistaking the sound of American motorcycle muscle, Frank burped the throttle, and the Harley responded, "I'm ready!" He grabbed the clutch, stomped the shifter, hit the throttle, and dumped the clutch, all in one precise, fluid motion.

The rear tire sent dust and gravel flying as the back end whipped around and fish-tailed down the long driveway. Frank held on tight; any more throttle, and the Harley would have won the wrestling match to be on top. At the end of the driveway came the first life-changing decision in this newfound independence. Turn right and head toward town; maybe lay low a couple of days to make the parents worry. That would show them I am not bluffing. Maybe I should go left toward the interstate. There was plenty of time for adventure. Graduation was just a ceremony anyway. If he didn't walk, the school could mail his diploma, no big deal. The freshmen football players did not have to report to the university for a couple of months. Plenty of time for adventure! Left it is! The old Steppenwolf song echoing in his head had become a checklist for Frank. Listening to the Harley's exhaust sing backup on the old rock song running through his head made Frank smile as he raced toward Interstate 80. "Time for a plan. Do I go left and head east, or right, and head west? I hear California and the Pacific Ocean are nice this time of year! West it is! Some would argue the West Coast is the best coast. I will find out!"

The spirits that had been struggling for control were ecstatic as they swirled in celebration around Frank's head. The very real fourth-dimensional battle had been raging for months undetected by the natural eyes of man over Frank's eternal soul. These vile creatures were so drunk with excitement over the thought of victory that they failed to notice the two immense angels of protection following in the distance. These Heavenly Warriors had been in many battles throughout history, and they knew this fight was far from over. They knew the Lord of the Heavenly Host had won the war over death and the grave. Despite being on the winning side, each knew they could not force their way into the situation without orders from the Captain of the Host. It is a decision every human must make for themselves. Frank, the Harley, and a dark horde of evil ones roared down the highway like a swarm of locusts, seeking to cause destruction. The horde, encircling, diving, and darting around the one they desired to destroy with as much collateral damage as possible. As for the Heavenly Warriors, right now, all they could do is hang back and await further orders. When the time arose, they would be ready to engage these vile creatures again. The war is already won, but every battle must be fought. And when the time was right and the orders given, they would be ready.

Chapter Three
Everything Will Be All Right!

Meanwhile, back on the farm, Joe and Sue came together on the porch. Joe wrapped his big ol' country boy arms around his lovely bride of almost twenty-five years. Tears streamed down both of their cheeks; they could hear the sound of the Harley as it faded in the distance. In Sue's ears, it sounded like the taunts of a seven-year-old on the playground, "Na-na-na-na-boo-boo; you can't catch me!" Joe searched for the right words to comfort her. "Sue, Darling, he'll be back tomorrow, Monday at the latest. You'll see. He just needs to cool off a little while."

Joe did his best to sound reassuring. "Baby, I know he's eighteen, but he can't come dragging in at noon or whenever he decides it's convenient!" Joe tried to suppress the anger in his voice. "This is every weekend lately, staggering in half-drunk or stoned; the Good Lord only knows what else he is into." Joe almost choked on his next words, "I saw what that lifestyle did to my daddy. . . ." Joe struggled and swallowed hard "It got him killed." The thought of losing his son ripped Joe's heart out. It felt like he had been sucker-punched in the gut and had every bit of wind knocked out of him.

"Joe," Sue looked up into his eyes, "He won't be back tomorrow. It is gonna take time for him to figure life out and find his way back. Until Jesus is real to him again, he doesn't know *the Way* home. . . ." Sue paused and sobbed into Joe's chest. "First, he has to get back on the right track; then, he will find his way back to us."

"Lord," Joe began, "We ask You to watch over and protect our little Tank." Joe struggled, not really knowing what to pray. Then he remembered the Scripture, ". . . and having done all, to stand. Stand therefore . . ." (Ephesians 6:13–14, KJV). "Lord, we stand on the promise You gave us in Your Word in Jeremiah 1:5."

Sue joined Joe as he struggled to pray, "'Before I formed you in the womb I knew you, before you were born I set you apart; I appointed you as a prophet to the nations'" (NIV). They both remember the revival meeting when the traveling evangelist spoke that Scripture over little six-year-old Frankie. They had prayed it countless times as a family through the years. As parents, each struggle in their heart to figure out, *What happened?* Desperately, both attempt in their mind to sort out where they had gone wrong. All they could do now was trust God and believe His Word to be true. They had tried to raise Frank in a Christian home and tried to be Christlike examples to their son. All of his life, they told him about the full armor of God. For now, in this battle, they had to believe Frank would find that armor and choose to put it on. Mom could not dress him for the battle ahead, and Dad could not fight it for him.

After many more tears, Joe bent down and kissed Sue's forehead, "It will be all right."

"I know." She whispered and sniffed, "I know."

"Besides," Joe said, trying to find a bright side, "We're supposed to go look at that Ford Tempo that Old Man Jenkins has out by the road for sale Tuesday."

Sue sniffed, snorted, and chimed in; her deep voice imitating Joe from an earlier conversation with Frank, "That Ford will make a fine car for college, good on gas, four doors to give all your friends a ride to class, and the brown color isn't so bad if you look at it in just the right light."

It was good to hear Sue laugh. Joe knew the heartache she was feeling—they both were feeling. They both also knew they could not rely on their own strength to get them through this stormy time.

Chapter Four
Barnfind

Joe went out to the barn, and Sue went back into the house, both tried to find something to occupy their minds. Each was hoping to do something similar to the usual Saturday routine. Joe picked up a piece of sandpaper to work on the China cabinet he was building as a surprise for Sue. With their twenty-fifth wedding anniversary just around the corner, he needed to take advantage of every spare moment. Besides, sanding was good therapy. Joe began sanding and let his mind go back to when Frank was a little boy. Well, when he was younger anyway. Frank had always been big for his age. He must have been maybe five or five and a half. Joe thought hard to remember, *Let's see; it was before Coach Tucker started with Frank the Tank in pee-wee football, which would have been age six. So five and a half would be about right. That young traveling evangelist was preaching up a storm, hellfire, and brimstone. He was really shucking the corn with a sermon that would make the pope come up front to rededicate his life.* Frank just sat drawing on the church bulletin; Joe and Sue were not paying much attention to him. They did not think he was paying attention to what was happening around him. He seemed to be in his own little world. That's when it happened. The organ player started playing the old hymn "Just As I Am." The young Southern evangelist shouted out with his heavy drawl, "It's time to come to Jeeesssuuusss!" Frank made a break for the front before anyone could stop him. "I'm coming, I'm coming. I'm ready to be bap-a-tized!" Frank ran up front and smiled a big ol' snaggletooth grin at the evangelist.

"I am gonna tell you one thing if this boy smiles any bigger, he's gonna bite his own ears off!" the evangelist chuckled and the whole congregation laughed.

Now, over a decade later, Joe let out a chuckle. He also realized he had been sanding the same spot all this time. The hairs on Joe's arm stood up as he remembered what happened next. Sue looked over at the masterpiece Frank had been working on so diligently on the back of the church bulletin. The center of the picture had the Cross with a stick figure of Jesus, and beside the Cross was another stick figure with tears coming from its eyes, with the word "sorry" written below. Sue picked up the masterpiece and quietly placed it in her Bible.

The same Holy Spirit presence that fell in that revival meeting over a decade ago began to fall on Joe in the barn as he encountered the edge of that unseen dimension. Countless numbers of Heavenly Worshippers encircled Joe singing, "Holy, holy, holy, LORD God Almighty" (Revelation 4:8, KJV). Even though humans may not see this dimension in the natural, it was easily accessed through prayer and praise. Falling to his knees, he remembered the prophecy spoken over Frank. "The Spirit of the Lord is upon you; He has anointed you to preach good news to the poor. He is sending you to bring healing to the brokenhearted, to proclaim liberty to the captives, to open the prison doors to those who are bound, to proclaim the year of our Lord (see Isa. 61:1). You, young fellow, will shout the good news of our Lord Jesus Christ to multitudes." Condemnation began to creep from the dark corner where he had been peering with beady red eyes fixed on his human target. He knew it would be risky with all the Holy Ones around, but he had managed to shoot a random thought of doubt between the ranks and into his victim's thoughts. Joe cried out; his heart felt as though it was being crushed, "Lord, I am sorry! I should have put a stop to this when I first saw it coming! Oh, Holy Spirit! Why didn't I listen to You? I let the gift you gave me slip away! It is all my fault."

The spirit of condemnation quickly slid across the floor, drew his flamberge, the weapon of choice in situations like this. Condemnation looked from victim to fiery-blade and back to victim as the light in the room dimmed ever so slightly. Now, his glaring eyes totally focused on Joe; he began to pry on the door to his target's mind, searching for that tiny sliver of an opening.

"This will be perfect," Condemnation hissed, "after all the emotion of today, he wantssss answersssss, and I'll give him answers!"

Sword, stained with the spiritual blood of countless victims, raised as Condemnation prepared to plunge it in and twist deep into the innermost part of Joe's spirit man, Condemnation forgot every other being in the barn and totally focused on the prize before him. "This is the stuff demon legends were made of. . . . to get a believer, *ha! I tell you what to believe*. . . . to stumble and . . ."

"Jesus, I need help! I am . . . I just don't know. Please show me what to do!" Then an indescribable peace flooded over Joe, faster than the human mind can even process. As light flooded the realm of the fourth dimension, a peace that the worldly human mind cannot even begin to understand surrounded him. Joe's desperate cries were heard in the Throne Room of the Most High God, and fourth-dimension events started to unfold.

"No! He called the name!" Condemnation shrieked as the name of the Holy One scorched his unholy ears. Joe knew the battle for his son will be tough, but suddenly he had all confidence—Jesus had already won the war. All Joe could do was stand and pray for the Lord to watch over Frank. In the unseen dimension, a huge Heavenly Warrior grabbed Condemnation by his slimy neck, spun him around, and placed his sword of Truth on the throat of his unholy foe.

"I know you haven't forgotten Romans already." The angel

gritted his teeth and exhaled. His breath was white-hot with the holiness that only comes from spending time in the presence of the Holy One. "Let me remind you; there is no condemnation, and that means you," deep voice reverberating throughout the spirit realm, "to them which are in Christ Jesus, who walks not after the flesh, but after the Spirit." The angel tossed Condemnation aside like a rag doll.

Condemnation went tumbling backwards. Trying to sound intimidating, he hissed, "I'm not finished."

"Today, you are done!" the angel roared, stopping him mid-sentence. "Now, go away!" The angel stepped aside, and Peace flooded into Joe's spirit. Condemnation zipped up through the rafters and away, knowing he would be no match for the Heavenly presences now flooding the barn.

Joe stood up, took a deep breath, and sighed, "Thank you, Jesus!" Feeling as though a huge weight had been lifted, Joe spent the rest of the afternoon puttering around the barn and doing light chores in the yard until suppertime. The angels of the Lord stood guard the rest of the afternoon, making sure that Condemnation, nor any other vile minion, interfered with the work that Peace was doing in Joe's spirit man. Whenever the Lord sent Peace to work in the life of a believer, the world cannot understand. Turmoil, Condemnation, Confusion, and several other demonic minions gathered in the distance, licking their battle wounds. They often argued over which one was the strongest, craftiest, vilest, or most evil. Seldom did they ever agree, but today each one knew the farm was off-limits.

"The best way to bring destruction to this group of humans . . ." an evil principality began with a hiss, "is through the young one. Destroy that one," the leader glanced toward Devastation, "and the other two will fall right behind!"

All present nodded in agreement, and a scruffy voice began, "Anger, Rage, and Doubt have a base camp set up with Bitterness digging a deep trench!" The self-appointed battle leader continued; no demon dared interrupt the strategist. "Lust and Perversion have also managed to get in through an unguarded door and put down roots. We all know Pride is already on the scene." A look of disdain swept across the general's face, and the demons all nodded in agreement.

"Maybe they can use our help!"

"Let's move out!"

Zip . . . Swoosh . . . Flash! All of the fallen ones took off faster than the speed of light; each of their tattered leather-like wings beat the air. They could not like each other, but they did have a common goal: finding Frank and wreaking havoc.

"Destroy the young one!" became the battle cry.

Chapter Five
Twenty-five Years: Seems like Yesterday

Meanwhile, Sue had gone inside and busied herself with Saturday chores. She cleared away the breakfast she and Joe had been enjoying when Frank came home. As a mom, she worried that her little boy had not eaten. Even if he was eighteen, Frank would always be her little boy. After cleaning the kitchen, she went to the living room and started straightening up and dusting. Sue's walk down memory lane began as she dusted the pictures on the stairway wall.

"Wow! Look at those kids," she snickered out loud, fondly remembering as she looked at their wedding picture. Sue and Joe were barely Frank's age when they got married. She could not believe that it was almost twenty-five years ago. She also remembered the first time she had seen the place they now called home. Joe's grandparents had given their only grandson and his new bride a thousand acres of prime farmland and a healthy nest egg as a wedding present. Joe and Sue did not consider themselves filthy rich, but money had never been a concern. She still had her breath taken away every time she pulled into the driveway. She had seen the property for the first time three days after she said, "I do" to the love of her life. In both cases, Joe and the property, it was love at first sight. They pulled off the highway in their pick-up with the ten-year-old silver Airstream in tow. They had to rough it for a couple of weeks while the water well was dug and the electric lines were run. Sue did not mind one bit; this was her small slice of paradise. Sue and Joe realized they had been truly blessed.

The plan was to live in the Airstream while Joe built Sue her dream home. "Baby, what kind of castle do I need to build for my queen?" Joe asked.

Sue answered without a moment's hesitation, "I would like a Walton house."

"A Walton house, what in the world is a Walton house?" Joe had a puzzled look on his face. Sue got all giggly with excitement as she started to explain her dream house. "There is a new show that comes on CBS channel four called *The Waltons*. It's a story about a family named the Waltons that takes place during The Depression."

Joe scratched his head, "You want me to build you a brand-new old house?"

"Yes, I absolutely love that old house! It is a big, white, wooden house with a huge porch across the front. It is a two-story, and it has those doghouse thingies on top."

"Hold on, woman!" Joe interrupted. "Now you are pulling my leg! How in the world are you going to make a dog sleep on the roof?"

Joe knew she was talking about dormers, but he was having way too much fun picking on his wife. "Wait; next, you are going to tell me it's not called the roof? It's called the ruff. Get it? The ruff, like ruff, ruff, a dog barking." Joe chuckled at his humor.

Sue stuck out her lip and acted like she was pouting, "You big meanie! You are making fun of me."

Every Thursday night, Joe would adjust the rabbit ear antenna on the GE porta-color, and they would watch *The Waltons*. Joe would sit with pencil and paper and take notes. Every Thursday night ended the same way. Sue would giggle, "Goodnight, Joe Bob." He would answer in mock disgust, "Goodnight, Sue Ellen."

Chapter Six
Home Sweet House

After a year and a half in the Airstream, Joe finally completed Sue's Walton-style dream house. They had watched countless episodes of the show. Joe always had pencil and pad in hand to put in all the extras he could glean from the few quick glimpses in each week's sixty-minute spot. He spared no expense to make everything as realistic as possible. The enormous two-story house was painted "old barnwood" gray and accented with white trim and porch railings. He made sure to include three dormers with scalloped trim, exactly like the ones on the home of the Waltons. He built the large porch across the front, complete with matching rocking chairs and a swing. Sue even planted rose bushes across the front and had Joe build a small shed for her garden tools that looked surprisingly like an old outhouse. Joe also added a windmill to complete the effect. He built a barn/shop to keep his lawn tractor in and to have a place to do his work. The house sat well back off the road with a long gravel drive and a white picket fence lining each side. A few years later, Joe built a huge barn down the road to store the farm equipment. He built it down the road, away from the house, because he did not want to mess up the postcard view of Sue's Walton house.

Joe and Sue had everything they wanted in their home except the pitter-patter of little feet. They both wanted a big family to fill up that big house. Sue was unsure if she wanted as many kids as the Waltons, but four, maybe five, would not be out of the question. She even joked about naming their first son John-Boy. After four discouraging years of trying to get pregnant, Sue's heart ached. Oh, how she longed to be a mother and have a family with the man she loved. She could imagine how Sarah, Abraham's wife, must have felt. Every time she was around family members, or when they went to town, or even when she and Joe went to church, inevitably, someone would ask, "When are you guys going to start a family?" She would hear comments like, "That's a mighty big house; you better get started if you are going to fill all those bedrooms." Or "How long are you going to make Joe wait to be a daddy?" There must be over a thousand ways to ask the same question. Sue knew no one intended their comments to be hurtful, but they pricked her deep within her heart. Somehow Sue always managed to smile and graciously answer, "We are patiently waiting on the Lord." Or "We are on the Lord's timetable." No one, not even Joe, knew the spiritual and emotional battle Sue was fighting in her head as well as in her heart. The final blow came when Sue went to see her ob-gyn.

The doctor's words echoed in her ears as her head filled with the thought of not bearing children of her own. "Sue, there is less than a ten percent chance you will ever get pregnant." He went on to tell Sue if she were ever able to get pregnant, she "would not be able to carry the baby to term." Sue felt like she was hit over the head, punched in the stomach, and had her heart ripped out, all at the same time. The sting of such devastating news made her want to cover her ears and run away screaming. The doctor tried to offer the option of adoption, but by that time, Sue had completely shut down, experiencing a total emotional overload. She did not hear another word after the doctor said she would never be able to carry a baby to term.

Sue was glad Joe had come with her for two reasons: She knew that there was no way she could drive home by the way she felt. More importantly, she was glad she would not have to repeat the horrible news the doctor had just given. His words were pounding in her head, like waves crashing against a crumbling pier during a storm. Sue felt like that pier, unsure how much longer she could hold it all together. Needless to say, it was a long, quiet ride home. Joe desperately searched his brain for the right words to comfort his grieving wife, but the words would not come.

Sue's heart longed for anything but silence. Inside she silently screamed, *Say something, anything.* Emotionally, she desired for Joe to reassure her that everything would be okay. *Just tell me you love me,* her heart longed to hear words that did not come. Joe's heart was also overwhelmed as he slid his hand across the seat and reached for the hand of his lovely bride.

No reaction, the lying visitor from the fourth dimension sprang into action, "That's not what she wants; you need to give her space and let her think." He slowly withdraws his hand.

"He can't even stand to touch me now that he knows I can't give him children." Deception turned his full attention toward Sue as they continued home. The uninvited demonic guest knew that right then, the silence was their best weapon. Rather than risk saying anything wrong, the dejected couple continued along in agonizing silence as the wedge of separation methodically drove between them, causing even more pain and heartache. The evil ones created countless false imaginations in the minds of their victims. As the humans rode in silence, hideous fourth-dimension beings darted around the vehicle. The sound of leather-like wings was deafening in the spirit realm. Deception, Rejection, Defeat, Hopelessness, even Bitterness, all dropped their small seeds in the form of idle thoughts into the soil of their victims' minds. Demonic laughter filled the unseen dimension around the car; to them, this was intoxicating.

Chapter Seven
The End

When they got home, Joe asked, "Would you like me to get you anything? I could make you supper if you would like."

"No thanks," Sue answered half-heartedly. "I am fine. I just need to lie down and rest for a bit."

Sue was anything but fine; the Father of Lies had already gone to work in the playground of Sue's mind. She headed to the bedroom, laid down, curling up into a fetal position, and began to cry her eyes out. The demon of deception strolls around the room like a predator, circling his prey; salivating, he took great pleasure picking apart the minds of these weak humans. Deception commenced to pound her mind like a boxer with a much weaker opponent against the ropes, "Joe doesn't love me." Deception circled and jabbed, "He wants a woman that can give him a son."

Deception followed with an uppercut, "Now that he knows I can't give him a child, he may never touch me again."

Sue's crying moved to wailing, and the demon kept feeding her thoughts, pounding away at everything in her mind. "If he loved me, he would be in here with me right now. How can he let me suffer all by myself?"

Jealousy slid his slimy, scaly green foot through the door that Deception had opened wide into Sue's mind to take a few shots while this human was pinned against the ropes of depression. "He did not think I noticed, but I saw him checking out that red-headed receptionist. I think she was flirting with him. I heard her whisper, "Call me if y'all need anything, darlin'." That little demon of deception was having a field day. He had totally blinded Sue and clouded what she had seen and heard. The flirty redhead was actually the doctor's seventy-year-old retired mother, who genuinely wanted Sue to call if she needed to talk to someone.

The demon of deception was having so much fun that he invited Doubt to join him. "God promised me a child; what did I do wrong? Maybe He doesn't love me! Maybe God is too busy for me!" The demons invited the spirit of suicide to join their party. The assignment was always the same: killing, stealing, and destroying as many human lives as possible. Usually, the smaller minions like Doubt, Depression, or Fear of Loss lurked around trying to find an opening into their victim's mind. As a spiritual being operating in the fourth dimension, demons sensed the tiniest opening into the battleground known as the human mind, then they began to circle like vultures. The demonic forces were all too aware that what the humans were deceived into thinking of as the final answer to all of life's problems—suicide—was just a quick step off the never-ending cliff of eternity.

"I'll go to the bathroom and take that bottle of sleeping pills. It will be simple; I'll just go to sleep and not wake up. Then Joe will be free to move on. He won't even have to bother filing for divorce."

If Sue could have looked over into the spirit realm, she would have seen the dark demon's fiery, red eyes, ablaze with excitement, swirling around her head, filling it with lies. The darkness and oppression were growing ever stronger and heavier in the bedroom to squelch any glimmer of light. Once the spiritual door was open for the first demon to get a foothold, he pushed, slithered, and finagled his way in to make room for as many of his fellow fallen ones as possible, trying to wreak havoc in every area of the human's life. Once legal access was granted, the darkness began to force out any hope or signs of "the Light." The victim was left pinned against the ropes, without even a glimmer of hope; there's no being saved by the bell, no referee to stop the fight. The forces of darkness continued to pound until the human was deceived into thinking suicide was their only solution. All these demons had been with their leader, the Father of Lies, since before the "Great Rebellion," getting them cast down from Heaven. Each had seen the glory of Heaven in the presence of the Holy One and knew the price they must pay for their rebellion. Their single goal and purpose: keep as many humans as possible from experiencing the glory they had lost. The heart may belong to the Holy One, but if they can win the war in the human mind, they had a shot at destroying their victim.

Chapter Eight
Battle in the Barn

While the enemy was waging war in Sue's mind, Joe was in the barn fighting his own battle in the spirit realm. Joe struggled with what to say to Sue. Sure, he wanted to have children, but the fact that they couldn't did not make Joe love Sue any less. Joe had gone to the barn because, in his mind, he is convinced Sue needed a little space and wanted to be left alone. As he sat in the barn, a slimy little demon of discouragement curled up on his shoulder and started whispering in his ear, "If I try to say something now, it will come out all wrong. I would likely make her cry and only make things worse."

Deception soon joined Discouragement, and they began working on Joe together. "I'm sure she needs time to think; if I crowd her, it will make things uneasy. She is probably resting, maybe taking a nap. I'll give her a little time; then we can talk about everything."

Little did Joe realize, the slimy little unseen demons on his shoulder, were buying time for the other evil spirits who were methodically at work in the house. The evil ones were very well aware of the damage two believers could do to the kingdom of darkness when they unite and pray. They planned to keep these two humans separated and convince Sue to destroy her life, thus setting into motion a spiritual domino effect of destruction that would affect countless lives. Joe sobbed into his hands as he knelt on the hard floor of the barn. Discouragement motioned to all of his minion friends that the coast was clear. Their leader, the old serpent, Satan, would be pleased if they could destroy both lives in a single afternoon. His work on the two original humans had affected all mankind throughout all of recorded time. Maybe, if they were successful today, their torment would be a little less severe, even if just for a moment. No telling how far the ripple effect from the destruction of these two humans might reach.

"Come on, all we need is a little crack." The little minion rubbed his slimy talons together, looking for a way into Joe's mind. The thought of destroying these humans made Discouragement salivate. What happened next took both human and non-human occupants of the barn by surprise.

Joe cried out, "Jesus, help me!"

In a blinding flash of light, demons went tumbling. "Oh no! Not Him!" The evil spirits that had been lurking, looking for an opening into the battleground of Joe's mind, scattered in every direction, well over the speed of light. The Holy Spirit flooded the barn and sent every manner of unrighteousness scrambling for the exits through walls and rafters. Joe later tried to describe what happened, "I felt two giant hands grab me by the shoulders and stand me straight up! Now, keep in mind, I knew I was in that barn by myself! I declare as sure as I'm talking to you right now, a voice told me, *Go to your wife now!* I cannot rightly say if it was aloud or in my head, but I had no doubt that I needed to go to Sue right then and there. I took off into the house as quick as I could go!"

The amazing part was what Joe could not see happening in the spirit realm. The split second the demons convinced Sue to end her life, Joe had called on the name of Jesus for help. In the spirit world, blinding light flooded the barn and sent the evil spirits that were hindering Joe scrambling, all over each other.

The exact moment the Holy Spirit flooded over Joe and sent him with a sense of urgency to Sue, Hope had slipped a small sliver into Sue's mind. "MY HOPE IS BUILT ON NOTHING LESS THAN JESUS' BLOOD AND RIGHTEOUSNESS!" she shouted. These words to the 100-year-old hymn filled the room." ON CHRIST THE SOLID ROCK I STAND" reverberated through the fourth dimension as beings of Light infiltrated the room. Blazing swords swooshing in every direction sent demons flying, falling, and fleeing. Joe threw open the door, and all he saw was Sue standing in the middle of the room, tears on her face with her arms raised. He could almost swear there was a glow around her.

As he looked deeply into her eyes, he spoke straight into her heart, "I love you with all my heart, now more than ever before. I love you now and forever."

She wrapped both arms around Joe and squeezed as hard as she could as she buried her head in his chest. She knew Joe loved her, and more importantly, she was a daughter of the Most High God. Everything was going to be all right. She could not believe she had entertained the thought of suicide, even for a moment.

Chapter Nine
Great Idea!

Several weeks later, just days after Thanksgiving, Sue was putting up a few Christmas decorations in the living room, and an idea came to her. Why hadn't she thought of it before, or had she? Was this a *déjà vu* moment? Sue was so excited; she danced around the living room, Santa ornament in hand, as joy filled her soul. She could hardly wait to tell Joe her fantastic idea when he came in from the fields. She heard the "squeak" as the brakes stopped Joe's old pickup in the driveway. She was about to bounce off the walls with excitement. "Hurry up, Joe!"

She had already made up her mind to wait for him in the house. *Slam!* went the door of the pickup. Sue giddily waited for what seemed like forever, "He must be moving in slow motion!"

Clomp, clomp, clomp, went his boots, finally on the front porch. *Click, click* as he opened the front door and stepped in. Sue could not hold it any longer, "We could adopt a baby, or maybe twins! Why not triplets?"

Joe felt like the unsuspecting victim of a surprise birthday party as he processed her words. The doctor had suggested this as a possible option when they last saw him. Joe assumed she had heard, and since she did not say any more about it, he had dismissed the idea. Sue squealed and clapped her hands quickly in front of her. She jumped in Joe's arms and started kissing his face. "Isn't that a wonderful idea?"

"Yes!" Joe answered, beginning to share her excitement. "It is a wonderful idea!"

"Goodie, now go wash up for supper!"

Joe quickly did as she said. They sat down to supper; it was all of Joe's favorites: fried chicken, green beans, mashed potatoes and gravy, homemade biscuits, and banana pudding for dessert. The only topic of conversation that night was adoption, with Sue talking and Joe smiling in agreement.

"Maybe we can get a sweet little girl or a precious little boy or one of each!"

Joe loved seeing Sue this excited about bringing children into their home. He finally piped in, "Maybe we could get five boys and have our own basketball team!"

Sue responded, "Don't be silly, Joe; that's five sets of diapers to change at once."

After supper, Sue cleaned and put away the dishes, and they got out the phone book and started looking for adoption agencies in the yellow pages. The next morning, Sue made the call and began the process: interviews, paperwork, phone calls, and more paperwork. Joe and Sue knew it would all be worth it, but it did not make the process any easier. The phone rang one afternoon with a possible candidate for adoption.

The agency representative said, "She is a young, unwed, expectant mother from Kansas that had come to Iowa to stay with relatives because her parents wanted to force her to get an abortion."

They both were so excited; in about six weeks or less, they would be parents. Tomorrow would be the initial meeting with the high school mother-to-be. Sue barely touched her supper; she attributed the queasy feeling to nerves.

"Joe, I am so nervous; I have butterflies in my stomach."

Joe grinned, "I know, tomorrow is a big day for us!"

They went to bed, and as Sue struggled to find sleep, Joe snored from a sound sleep. Sue tossed and turned, trying desperately to find rest. "Mr. Sandman, where are you? Please bring me some sleep!"

The butterflies began to tap dance in Sue's stomach; about 2:45 a.m., the butterflies went into all-out rebellion. *Swoosh!* Sue threw back the covers and dashed for the toilet, "Oh, God! No, not a stomach virus!" The sudden drop in temperature, due to the rapid removal of covers, caused Joe to awaken from his deep sleep. He followed her to the bathroom and asked, like men often do in situations like this.

He said, "Baby, are you okay?" as he held Sue's hair away from her face. He realized it was a dumb question when it left his lips, confirmed by her glance over the shoulder between heaves. Obviously, she was not doing well. Joe had never known Sue to be this sick; he could not ever remember her being sick in all their years of marriage.

The following day, a trip to the doctor and a pregnancy test confirmed baby Frank was on the way. The doctor warned, "Sue, this is an extremely risky pregnancy, not only for the baby, but your life could also be at risk. You do have the option of terminat—"

"No!" she stopped him, "Absolutely not! That is not even an option!"

"Sue, as your doctor, I think you should consider your own health and life—"

Sue stopped him again, "Doc, it will be all right!"

Joe and Sue later got word, when they called to reschedule, "The young, green-eyed, redhead from Kansas had decided to go home and keep her little girl." She was born two weeks after they found out baby Frank was on the way.

Now, almost nineteen years later, all Sue could do was stand on God's promise, "It will be all right!" She repeated this to herself over and over. Sue and Joe had done their best to raise Frank in a Christian home. Now, he had to choose the path he would take.

Chapter Ten
Go West!

Frank hit I-80 headed west. The weather was perfect, not a cloud in the sky. It was a very pleasant seventy-five degrees outside. Frank smiled; this was a great day to ride, clear his head, and enjoy his newfound freedom. He would ride the few miles to the Big I-80 truck stop and fill up the Harley's tank and his stomach. He was feeling a little hungry since he never made it to the table for breakfast. Frank was glad the annual Truckers Jamboree was still over a month away, so it would be normal traffic in and out. All those trucks around could make a biker a little nervous. He was able to pull right up to the pump and top the Harley's five-plus gallon tank off. He was glad Mr. Stone had helped him stretch the tank; an extra gallon would help put that much more distance between him and dad. Frank went inside, paid for the gas, a burger, and a drink. He walked out, choked down lunch, pulled on his helmet, and gave the Harley a kick.

Frank took a minute to think about his next move, "I can head back toward town. . . . maybe go crash at Toby's and party for a few days. Dad wouldn't have a clue; let them worry for a few days, then head home. Or—option two—really do it! Hit the road and head west!"

The spirit of pride that had come along for the ride whispered in Frank's ear, "Time to be a man; if you go back now, you will always be their little boy. Dad will never see you as a man."

Frank eased away from the pump, watching for trucks, and headed toward I-80. Pride had once again done his job. Once he was given an open door into a person's mind, he could plant a thought so deeply that the person would believe they'd come up with it on their own, and it must be the right thing to do. The spirits were doing everything they could to push Frank farther down the road to self-destruction. They knew the best way to accomplish their goal: get Frank out from under Joe and Sue's physical roof and out from under the spiritual covering their home offered.

"California is the place I ought to be!"

Frank laughed at his humor; he loved watching *The Beverly Hill-billies* reruns as a kid, but now was the time to be a man. Pride and Anger dug their invisible talons into Frank's brain, and his head began to pound. He screwed down on the throttle, and the Harley let out a loud *"Leeeetttt'ssss Gooooo!"*

Pride really started to work his magic: "I don't need them, and I can make it on my own. I am an all-state linebacker. Look at me, six foot four, 240 pounds. I look decent. Who am I kidding; I look marvelous! I'll head to Hollywood to be a movie star; I can easily find a job. They will be beating down my door. Maybe, I'll stop by Las Vegas for some adult entertainment because I am a man, and I make my own rules now!"

Lust dug his talons deep into Frank's brain, planting images from the porn he had been watching over the last few months. Frank screamed out as he headed west, "Woohoo! This is great! No more of the old man's rules! Hell, I may never go back to Iowa! If it feels good, do it! Right now, life is good, so let's go do it!"

Chapter Eleven
Remembering an Old Friend

The Harley was running great; the hum of the American Muscle V-twin was relaxing, almost therapeutic. *Wish Mr. Stone were here,* Frank thought, *he would understand. He knew what it was like to live life outside of Iowa.*

Frank had known Mr. Stone ever since he could remember. Mr. Stone had been around the church, and everyone in town knew him. If you had something broken, he could fix it. And if Mr. Stone couldn't fix it, it didn't need to be fixed! He owned a junkyard/auto shop on the north end of town. When you brought your vehicle to his shop, you could trust him to fix it right and not overcharge.

Mr. Stone shared his story with anyone who would listen. He had spent the early part of his adult life as an army grunt. He had been born on a farm, just a few miles from where Frank lived now.

"My daddy served in World War II," Mr. Stone always began the same way, clearing his throat. "He was my hero." He would give a half-smile. "I wanted to be an army man like my daddy as far back as I could remember."

As he rode, Frank could almost hear Mr. Stone's rough gravelly voice say, "I could not wait to get off the farm and out of Iowa, so I lied about my age and enlisted when I just turned seventeen."

Mr. Stone would continue, his big barrel chest expanding slightly with pride. "Times were tough on the farm," he would continue, "so this was a good opportunity for me to get away and see the world! No sooner had I finished basic than the President of these United States decided we needed to help out in Korea."

Frank remembered him talking about turning eighteen and then nineteen on foreign soils. "Boys," he would tell the Junior High Sunday School class, "I was hooked on army life and all kinds of drugs when Vietnam rolled around. I loved the action and the thrill of it all. I thought I was invincible!"

Mr. Stone always got really serious when he shared this part of his testimony. "I saw things I wanted to forget and did things I started to regret; it was a crazy time. I remember sitting, leaning on a tree trunk; we had been up about thirty hours or more. Artillery shells were exploding all around. I had seen my buddy Gillis taken out the day before by a sniper. He was sitting there talking, having a smoke, then he just slumped over—never finished his sentence or his smoke." Mr. Stone would clear his throat and wipe his eyes as he seemed to relive that moment every time he told this story. "That's when I knew I was not invincible! I remembered the preacher's words from when I was a boy. He would talk about how everybody had sinned. I knew some of the stuff I had done was definitely sin, then the preacher said, 'The payment for sin was death.' I could see death all around me. He said, 'If we died in that sin, we would be separated from God, forever, in a place called Hell.' The preacher said Hell was worse than any place we could imagine on Earth. I knew if Hell was worse than what was right in front of me, I did not want any part of it. No, sir, not at all! The preacher said Jesus had paid that price for me."

Then a big smile would come over Mr. Stone's face, "So, in that jungle, leaning with my back against that tree, I asked Jesus to forgive me and gave Him control of my life. Boys, I didn't fully understand why God did not immediately suck me up out of that jungle and back to Iowa, but I knew things were different on the inside, in my head, and most importantly, in my heart. I promised the Good Lord if He would get me home safe and sound, I would take every chance He would give me to share this story and praise His name!"

Chapter Twelve
Time to Build a Bike

Frank wiped the moisture from his eyes as he rode on and remembered his old friend Mr. Stone. Yep! Mr. Stone was the *real deal*. He loved to talk about anything with a motor, but his real passion was sharing what Jesus had done in his life. He was the same at the shop as he was around the church. "He didn't just wear religion on Sunday; he lived Jesus every day!" Frank nodded toward the sky. "If there is a place called Heaven, I know you are there, Mr. Stone!" He rode on, remembering his friend.

Mr. Stone decided to hang up the combat boots after twenty-five years and two wars. "I had seen all the world I wanted to see; now it is time to go home." He returned to his hometown in Iowa and bought Smitty's garage from Old Man Smith. He joined the small church in town and volunteered to teach a Sunday school class full of rowdy Jr. High boys. All of the boys loved to go to Mr. Stone's class; they all respected him. He may have been a little rough around the edges, with huge calloused hands and skin like tanned leather. After thirty seconds around him and one look into his twinkling blue eyes, the love of Christ in him would be revealed.

Frank remembered how, as he got older and started high school, he would spend Saturdays hanging around the shop with Mr. Stone. He enjoyed it because the local hot rodders would swing in to visit or work on their cars. Mr. Stone did not allow any foolishness as he called it: no alcohol, drugs, or foul language. If someone came in and needed a part from the salvage yard, Mr. Stone would pay Frank a couple of dollars to pull the part. Anytime Mr. Stone would be working on something, he took the time to show Frank how to do it right. Frank remembered one Saturday when he was in tenth grade.

"Boy, you spend all this time around working on other folk's stuff. It's time we build you something of your own."

Frank did not know at the time, but Mr. Stone had already run the idea past Dad and Mom; of course, Mom did not like the idea of a motorcycle.

"I have enough old bikes around here for you to put together a nice ride of your own. I'll let you do the work yourself, and I'll make sure you don't build something that will get you killed. It is a fine thing to ride something you put together with your own hands." Mr. Stone knew his stuff when it came to putting a bike together, especially Harleys.

Frank remembered all of the time and effort they put into the bike he was now riding. Mr. Stone was right, "It was a fine thing to ride something built with your own two hands." He knew what he wanted to build as soon as Mr. Stone had given him free rein of the bike boneyard. He had been eyeing the early seventies Sportster frame for a while. Frank really liked the springer front end. He remembered how he wanted so badly to put twenty-six-inch ape hanger handlebars on it. "Mr. Stone, those handlebars will be cool on my bike. See, look at this picture."

"That is it exactly, a magazine bike. You ride that thing down the road, and if you don't kill yourself, your arms will be ready to fall off after a few miles. Even a boy your size does not need over a sixteen to eighteen-inch bar. That way, you can look cool and still enjoy riding your bike."

After a couple of hours of riding, he realized Mr. Stone was right.

He had a one-of-a-kind bike. His Harley had the look of a sixties-style chopper but the power and ride of an eighties-style touring bike. They had even put an electric starter on it, but Frank always preferred the kick start. As he looked down on the large five-plus gallon tank with its hand-rubbed black lacquer paint job, he could have sworn he saw Mr. Stone looking back at him. He was even glad they had put the sissy bar he initially thought looked stupid because it was perfect for attaching the duffle bag securely.

Chapter Thirteen
Life Is Good; Distance Is Better

Frank continued down the road to put as many miles as possible between him and his dad before dark. Less than a year earlier, he and Mr. Stone were putting the finishing touches on the bike. He remembered how happy he was to have his Harley for his senior year of high school.

"Life was good!"

He had been an all-district defensive player his junior year, and the whole town was excited for football season to start. Everyone was expecting another championship season. He and Stacy, the best-looking girl in school, had started dating. The college scouts had already started showing an interest.

"Life was better than good; it was great!" Frank did not realize it yet, but that is when life began to spiral out of control.

Chapter Fourteen
Death Stinks

"Frank, could you come in here?" Mr. Stone called him to come into the office less than a week after they finished the bike. "I need to talk to you about something important." He spoke with a solemn look on his face.

"What is it? Did I mess up something? What did I do wrong?"

"It is all right, Frank. You did not do anything wrong or mess anything up." Mr. Stone gave a half-hearted chuckle. "I just need to talk seriously to you for a minute. I had a doctor's appointment this morning, you know."

"Yes, sir, I remember you saying something the other day. Is everything all right?" Frank asked.

"Well . . ." followed by a long pause, "no, not really."

"What's the matter? Are you sick? You look fine!" Frank could tell by the look on Mr. Stone's face that everything was not all right. Mr. Stone continued in a strange, unsteady manner that caught Frank off guard. Mr. Stone was a rough man, slightly shorter than Frank but broader across the shoulders.

"The doc said I needed to call my family together, and you are about the closest I got to family. He said I got cancer in my pancreas."

Frank stammered, "Mr. Stone, they got places that deal with . . . you know . . . that specialize in treating ummm . . ."

"It's okay, Frank. You can say cancer; it's not contagious."

"Okay, well, what are you going to do? Are they gonna give you that chemo stuff or what?" Frank was desperately looking for an answer.

"Frank, I want you to listen closely for a minute; what I got to say ain't easy. The doc says with this kind of cancer, when they find it, it's usually too late to do anything about it."

Frank could see tears forming in Mr. Stone's eyes as he spoke. "The doc says maybe a month or two at best."

"No! You can't die!" Frank felt a flood of emotions come over him. What he felt most was anger. "I can't let you die! God can't let you die! We just need to pray! All my life, my parents, the preacher, and you, everybody talks about God and His love; if He is real, He can fix it. He can make you well; He has got to. . . ."

"Frank, listen. God is in control; He is ready for me, and I feel a peace that everything is going to be all right!" Mr. Stone took Frank by the shoulders and looked him in the eyes.

"No, Mr. Stone. I refuse to let you go!" Frank pulled away. He hopped on the Harley and took off down the street. It seemed like the things he had been taught about God were being challenged. He had never really had anyone close to him pass away. He prayed with all his might that God would spare Mr. Stone. Frank did not realize that God was ready to call Mr. Stone home, and he was prepared to go.

Two weeks later, the headline read: "Local Army Hero Passes Away Quietly in Sleep." Almost the whole town turned out to pay their final respects to Mr. Stone in his dress blues with a chest full of medals and hardware from the years he had given to his country. Frank was the most noticeable absence. While others mourned, he burned with rage. Frank could not bring himself to go to the funeral. Instead, he went to a field to clear his head and his heart. How could God let this happen?

"I thought You healed people! How could You let him die? I

believed in You. I prayed. I believed in my heart. . . ." He shook his fist toward the sky. "I hate You, and I don't need You anymore. I just asked for one small thing. I don't have time for a God that doesn't have time for me!" That was when the door cracked open into Frank's spirit man. The fourth dimension was buzzing with activity around Frank in that moment of hurt and heartache. Bitterness quickly slipped into Frank's mind and slid his slimy foot straight into the open door of his heart. Deception was next into Frank's mind, knowing in his current state, Frank's mind would quickly be able to convince his heart that the things he knew as a kid to be true had all been a lie. Deception knew that if he could begin to cast the slightest shadow of doubt on a believer's faith, in their natural mind, it was just a matter of time before total disbelief took over.

"Now, to avoid any interference from the Holy Ones . . ." The thought of facing Truth made Deception shutter "Oh, well, we have the advantage now. . . . We have got to take it!" All the dark forces agreed with Deception and went to work on their latest target.

In the nine months since the funeral, a multitude of demons had set out to send him down the road that leads to destruction. Once Bitterness began to take root, he invited Anger, Rage, and Deception. Anger would constantly irritate Frank's spirit like a splinter under the skin that is not easily removed. Anything dealing with God, the Bible, or church would agitate him. On the other hand, Rage was like an active volcano, bubbling below the surface, ready to erupt and spew all over anything in his path without warning. Frank now had an overwhelming desire to try everything he had been raised to call sin. Deception continued to drive an invisible wedge between Frank and his Heavenly Father, who, more than anything, desired reconciliation.

The spirits of anger and resentment had ripped open that wound in Frank's heart again as he rode down the interstate and remembered all of the emotions he had gone through less than a year earlier. Bitterness had taken a deep root over the last several months: *"How could God let this happen?"*

Doubt dug its talons in and whispered in Frank's mind, "If God were real, He would have saved your friend. Maybe He was too busy or distracted to hear your prayers."

Arrogance chimed in, "God only has as much power as you give Him! He is just a crutch for kids to help them sleep at night; only a weak mind needs a crutch! I am strong, and I have a strong mind. I don't need my parent's religion anymore!"

Frank thought the fresh air was helping him clear his head; however, the opposite was happening. The spiritual doors that had only opened a small crack were now kicked wide open, and all types of evil spirits were playing in Frank's mind. They took turns swooping in and out of the battleground of Frank's mind, spewing all sorts of vile blasphemy. The mental torment was almost unbearable. He wanted to pull his hair out, scream, hurt somebody. . . . do something . . . anything to make the pressure in his head go away.

The two huge angelic beings maintained their distance; as tough as it was, they had to hang back and watch as the mental assault continued.

"Why doesn't Frank just call out to the Way?" the first Heavenly Warrior spoke, thinking out loud.

"The humans are always seeking their own way or trying to find another way."

"They can't find peace until they know the Prince of Peace!"

"I know, but I just . . . I want to . . . well . . ."

"I know you want to ruffle some demon wings, but you know the rules!"

"I know we can't act on our own, without orders!" These two-winged warriors are veterans of many fourth-dimension conflicts, and both know they cannot interfere without orders and proper prayer support.

Chapter Fifteen
That Was Close

F rank rode on for a couple of hours and decided that the west side of Des Moines would be a good place to stop, stretch his legs, and fill the tank. He picked up a map from the gas station and began to chart a course for adventure. *Let's see; we should be good on the gas until around Omaha. We can refuel there and get something for supper.* He pulled in for his final gas and food stop after another uneventful couple of hours or so.

Now, he would make the easy ride over to Fort Kearney for the night; according to the map, it was only a little over an inch. Fort Kearney's campground would be perfect for Frank's first night of independence. Frank hopped back on the Harley and hit the inter-state for the last leg of today's adventure. He let his mind drift off to camping trips and family vacations as a kid. "Are we there yet? How much longer?" All the questions kids usually whined from the back-seat. Now, he was almost looking forward to the public shower at the campground to wash off the day's worth of road grime. The weather had been perfect all day with no summer showers. The temperature was seventy degrees, perfect for riding. He leaned back against his duffle bag; everything was perfect. This was the life, so relaxing (ah, deep breath), could it get any better?

Wamp! Wamp!

"Oh, crap! Where did that eighteen-wheeler come from?" The truck had come up behind Frank and changed lanes to pass. In his daydreaming state of mind, Frank had also begun to drift to the other lane in front of the truck. At the sound of the horn, Frank jerked the handlebars and swerved back to the right lane. The truck passed so closely; Frank could have touched the passenger side door handle. *Swoosh!* The truck and trailer flew past; the rushing wind of eighty thousand pounds of steel and wheels caused the bike to wobble slightly. Out of reflex or fear or whatever, he gave the trucker half a peace sign as the volcano of rage was ready to erupt.

"If that worthless son of a booger stops, I'm gonna . . ."

Seeing Frank's reaction, the driver eased his right rear trailer tires off the edge of the road and gave Frank a dust and debris shower at seventy miles per hour.

Rage would have liked nothing more than to pound the driver in the ground, but common sense reminded the Harley rider that he was no match for a fully loaded eighteen-wheeler at highway speeds. The driver did a quick brake tap, and Frank backed off the throttle to avoid biting a back bumper. He decided it was best to let the trucker get a ways ahead. The trucker was now gone, out of sight, but not out of mind. Evidently, he felt it would be best to get on the C.B. and share their previous adventure with his buddies. Over the next thirty miles or so, every time a trucker saw Frank, they gave a loud blast on their air horn. Some pointed, laughed, and grabbed the mic to share adventures over the C.B. airwaves. Other truckers made goofy faces and returned Frank's half-peace sign salute. All of these shenanigans made Frank's blood boil. Anger was working overtime. If he could have five minutes with any one of them, or all of them, it didn't matter. Frank could feel the rage as his temples throbbed, "I just want to hurt somebody!"

Frank was glad to see the Highway 44 sign, Exit 272, just a few more miles. Finally, his exit, Frank eased over, touched the brakes, and upshifted. The V-twin's pipes sounded like the Mormon Tabernacle Choir singing the "Hallelujah Chorus." Frank headed south a couple of miles, then turned east for a few more miles down the highway that appeared to have been carved through the fields of sprouting corn stalks. Frank knew, having lived his entire life in the "corn belt," harvest time was still a couple of months away. Then, that sea full of green stalks would be bustling with activity. There it was, his sign, Fort Kearney State Recreation Park. It had been several years since he had been here, but he remembered where the office was to check in. He stopped and paid a couple of bucks for his spot, then headed toward the bathhouse.

Chapter Sixteen
Sunset on the First Day of Freedom

As the sun began to set on his first day of freedom, Frank knew he had less than an hour to settle in before dark. The first priority for Frank was a nice hot shower. He was starting to smell himself, and he knew from the reaction of the desk clerk, she could smell him as well. He pulled up and stopped next to the bathhouse and unhooked the duffle bag. It might not be a bad idea to bring it inside. There were not many campers around since most of the kids were still in school, but let's not take any chances. He stepped into the damp, musty-smelling bathhouse. Yep, just like he remembered. The sound of dripping water, despite all physical efforts of previous occupants, that dripping faucet could not and would not be silenced. He stripped down, "Dang it; I forgot to get soap and shampoo." He stepped into the shower stall; someone had left half a bar of soap.

At first, the thought was disgusting, then, maybe not so bad. Frank reached for the hot water tap and gave it three-quarters of a turn. He was not prepared for the arctic blast that gushed out. Frank stepped back to allow the water to reach a more acceptable temperature. He also notices that he had a shower mate, a grey tree frog that caught Frank off guard when he jumped from his perch near the shower head. Once the water reached an almost lukewarm temperature, he grabbed the soap between his thumb and forefinger. He held it under the shower stream to wash away any jungle rot the previous owner may have left behind.

"We cannot have body parts falling off as we ride to freedom, now can we?" He chuckled at his twisted sense of humor.

He finished his shower, got dressed, and set out to find his lodging for the night. He eased the Harley along the campground road; there it was, site number forty-nine, right by the back lake, just like Marg at the front desk said. A picnic table and rusty grill were close by, not that Frank had anything that needed to be heated, and a restroom was within walking distance. Frank thought aloud, "Home sweet home, for the night anyway. Tomorrow we will get up with the sun and head west with the wind in our face and the sun on our back."

Frank gathered up some sticks, took out his lighter, and got a small fire going in the grill. Then, he fished out the snacks he had picked up at his last stop. After supper, he rolled out his bedroll and started settling down for the night, the moon providing just enough light. Now, Frank was ready for a good night's rest. He fidgeted around with the bedroll, struggling to make himself as comfortable as possible.

"Great!"

Frank could hear a wild party, complete with loud music and whooping and hollering in full swing across the way. Any other time, he would love to go party with his neighbors, but not tonight. Despite the loud music, Frank faded off to sleep in a few minutes. Frank assumed the ranger must have shown up sometime after midnight because he noticed the music fade about that time.

"What was that?"

Something or someone startled Frank awake. Frank may have been asleep, but the demons traveling with him were wide awake, ready for action, and quickly had his adrenaline pumping. He laid still and listened. It didn't take long to remember where he was.

"Shhh! There is his motorcycle, Bobby!" Frank heard an attempted whisper.

"I know! I ain't that drunk; I can see it."

Frank squinted to see in the predawn light. There they were, two guys, about twenty-five yards away. They had not figured out where he was yet. Frank did not know their intentions but was fairly certain they weren't coming to welcome him to the campground.

"That's fine," Rage stirred in Frank. "These two knuckleheads are about to get way more than they bargained for!"

"What are we going to do again, Johnny?"

"We are going to rough him up a little; you know he's the one that went and got the Park Ranger!"

"Yeah! We can take his money and buy more beer too!"

Frank could feel his blood boil; Rage began to take over. His heart started to pound in his chest; he could feel the adrenaline rush, and he liked it. The evil ones around Frank were in a frenzy; they loved it when the humans set out to inflict harm on one another. The volcanic rage within Frank began to boil as he eased around on his bedroll and prepared to defend himself. In all actuality, Frank was preparing to teach *stupid* a lesson.

Bobby and Johnny had not figured out exactly where he was due to the combination of low light and too much partying the night before. "There he is! He is still asleep! I'll snatch him up, and you hit him in the gut with the bat. Then we'll both work him over and take his wallet. He'll never know what hit him!"

The not-so-dynamic duo did not realize, not only was Frank wide awake, but he could also hear every word they were unsuccessfully trying to whisper. Just as Bobby bent over to "snatch him up," Frank came up with a left foot to Bobby's midsection, making his lungs temporarily forget their number one job, to breathe. Frank rolled as Johnny swung and grazed his shoulder with the Louisville Slugger. Frank, still feeling the rush and embracing it as it intensified his anger, landed the first blow to the ribs, then another, and another.

Finally, a shot to the jaw and Frank could have sworn he heard the jawbone crack. With Johnny out of the picture, he turned his attention to Bobby, still struggling to catch his breath. With the threat eliminated, Rage was erupting; it was about causing as much pain as possible.

Crunch

Frank could feel the cartilage of Bobby's nose get squishy as he landed the first of a series of blows to the face. Frank's fourth-dimension traveling companions were ecstatic. They shrilled, whooped, and hollered in tones unheard by human ears. In less than forty seconds, the two would-be attackers had been rendered unconscious.

Frank reached for the bat. "Finish them!" Murder had joined the party and was screaming in his ear. "Fingerprints." One of the huge, angelic guardians swooped in, dropped a thought, and backed out before even the forces of evil could notice. Frank decided it would be best to move along earlier than planned in case Johnny and Bobby's party buddies came looking for them. The sun would start to rise in less than an hour, so he better get moving. He hefted Bobby over his shoulder and headed off toward the restrooms. He set him down behind a trash dumpster and headed back for Johnny. Johnny stirred a little, so Frank gave him a kick to the side, and back out he went. He trudged back through the woods and placed Johnny a few feet from his once partner in crime. Frank suddenly remembered what he had learned watching *Miami Vice* and grabbed the bat with a rag, careful not to leave any prints. He put it between them, hoping with any luck, everyone would think Bobby and Johnny had beaten up each other. Maybe they were too drunk to remember anything different.

Frank rolled up his bedroll, shoved it in the duffle bag, and strapped it to the Harley just as the sun was breaking the horizon. He gave the Harley a quick kick and eased out of the Fort Kearney Recreational Area as quietly as the V-twin would allow. He still had about half a tank of fuel, so he would try to put a few miles between himself and the campground, just in case the authorities got involved. At six in the morning on a Sunday, the traffic on the highway back to Interstate 80 was nonexistent. There was hardly any traffic on the interstate as well. As he rode along, thinking about what had happened a little over an hour ago, he looked down and noticed blood on his hands from Bobby's obviously broken nose.

"Silly, Bobby. Kicks are for, well, for you, Bobby. . . ." He laughed an insane laugh; right now, he was the funniest person he knew. As Frank rode on and the adrenalin rush wore off, he realized there was a nice slight bruise where the Louisville Slugger had made contact. As he stretched his shoulder out, Frank laughed again, "Mr. Stone was right. The twenty-six-inch ape hangers would definitely not be a good idea right now!"

Chapter Seventeen
Back on the Farm

Joe and Sue each went about their usual Saturday routine, both finding it hard to focus on anything other than their son. Both of them felt as though they had lost their son. Their feelings were similar to the feelings of grief a person has when someone they love passed away. Not only was Frank running from them, but he was also running from God. They spent the next few hours praying for their son, remembering Frank as a child and growing up, as well as trying to make sense of it all. "Where had they gone wrong? What else could they do? How could they have prevented this?"

Sue heated up leftovers for supper. They each made idle chit-chat about what they had accomplished that day.

"I finally got that section of fence repaired, and then I nailed that loose tin down on the backside of the barn." Joe tossed his comment out to make conversation over supper.

Sue responded, "I was able to clean out the junk closet. I got two or three boxes of stuff that can go to the rummage sale they're having in town."

"You aren't giving away any of my priceless heirlooms, are you?"

Joe responded, feigning a look of seriousness. "I've got at least five, maybe six dollars' worth of stuff in that old closet!"

"Joe, it is for a good cause!"

"Well, I suppose I could be persuaded to part with these treasures!" Joe deepened his voice, wrinkled his brow, and puckered his lips out as if contemplating the matter in a most serious manner.

Sue had avoided the elephant in the room long enough, "Joe, I hope he's all right! I pray he doesn't do something foolish and hurt himself—or worse."

"I'm sure he's fine. He might surprise us and show up at church in the morning. If not, we will see his friends. I'm sure some of them know where he is." Joe did his best to sound reassuring. Oddly enough, at that very moment, he prayed, "Lord, we thank You for watching over Frank. We ask you to send your angels to watch over him and keep him from harm."

Joe prayed. He did not fully understand, but out of obedience, Joe offered up a quick prayer.

Unknown to anyone in the natural world, as Joe prayed, God had released the two giant angels, traveling in the distance behind Frank, on Interstate 80 in Nebraska. At the very moment when Frank began to drift into the other lane, in front of a passing trucker, Joe asked God to place a hedge of protection around Frank. The first angel altered the course of the truck and the Harley, who were only a few inches apart by flying between them at the last second. The second angel helped the trucker blast his air horn and encouraged him to dust Frank and not throw on the brakes in front of Frank. Had the trucker listened to Rage, instead of Peace, and the latter occurred, Frank would have eaten the back bumper of the trailer at seventy miles per hour.

They finished supper with more chit-chat, then cleaned the dishes and put everything away. Joe and Sue headed to the living room to try and relax and watch TV. Joe flipped through the channels, not finding anything of interest, while Sue sat quietly, trying to read. Every time the dog would bark, she would stretch to see out the front window. Sue hoped at any second to hear the rumble of the Harley coming up the driveway. After reading and rereading the same page a dozen times, Sue realized she wouldn't be able to focus enough to make any progress beyond chapter one.

"I am going to bed," Sue said in a low voice.

Without saying a word, Joe clicked the remote off and followed her to the bedroom. They each got ready for bed and climbed under the covers. Joe reached and turned off the bedside lamp; they prayed together and said goodnight.

"Hold me, Joe," Sue whispered, as she laid her head on his shoulder. He stretched his arms around her. Neither one of them was quite sure how things would turn out; they just believed everything was going to be all right. They were both up the next morning before the alarm went off, not well-rested at all.

Joe acted like he didn't notice Sue peek out the window to see if the Harley was parked in its usual spot. He had already checked Frank's room. Both secretly hoped he had snuck in during the night. Deep down, they knew he had not. Sue made a light breakfast as Joe looked over the Sunday school lesson again. They puttered around the house getting ready, and when it was time, they left for church. As they pulled into the parking lot, Joe and Sue glanced around for Frank or the Harley; no sign of either. They looked at each other and put on their *it's all good* church face. They had gotten to the adult Sunday school class early enough to drink coffee, eat doughnuts, and fellowship, just like every week. Joe and Sue were in a room full of some of their closest friends, yet they both felt they could not share what was going on. Maybe it was their pride or embarrassment; whatever the case, Joe and Sue did not feel like they could share, not right now anyway. When it came time for prayer requests, Joe vaguely asked the group to pray for Frank and the decisions he was facing. This way, everyone assumed it was decisions about where to attend college. Joe felt like the more people praying, the better, even if they weren't praying specifically. At least prayers were being offered. After all, Frank had several scholarship offers to play football, and if people assumed, well, in Joe's mind, that was okay too. Frank had done very well playing the church game in the eyes of the adults since Mr. Stone passed away. He had maintained the appearance of a good little church boy on Sunday, but during the rest of the weekend, Rebellion was in control. Only the young people close to Frank knew what was going on in his secret life of partying and rebellion.

Chapter Eighteen
Sunday, Sunday

Joe and Sue Carter loved Cornerstone Church. They had attended since they were first married, almost twenty-five years ago. Originally, it was a Baptist church built in the late 1800s. The current 400-seat, red-brick auditorium had been built in the 1950s. When Joe and Sue joined the church, the pastor was Mark Kirkpatrick, known to everyone as Dr. Kirkpatrick, theological expert. Most would consider him an uptight Baptist preacher in his mid-sixties. After the first Sunday, the newlyweds attended, Joe and Sue questioned, "Is this really where God wants us?"

"Joe, that place is like a . . . I don't know. . . . I can't come up with the words. The people seem so unhappy."

"I know what you mean. . . . the preacher . . . It feels like he is talking at the people and not to the people."

The couple prayed and felt as though God had led them to this church, and they should give it a little time. Within the next two months, things started happening around that church. It began when the pastor went to a conference and met up with a couple of brothers from seminary. They started talking to Dr. Kirkpatrick about being filled with the Holy Spirit and the gifts of the Spirit. Dr. Kirkpatrick struggled with that thought, as he later shared with the congregation from the pulpit, "I returned home after the conference, still trying to wrap my brain around the idea. All my life, I had been taught. . . . I even taught that the gifts of the Spirit had passed away with the disciples. I believed with all my heart that Jesus had sent the Holy Spirit temporarily to help the early church get started. I was wrong!"

He continued, tears flowing down his elderly cheeks. "The other night, two nights ago, I lay in bed struggling with this idea. I called out to the Lord. I said, 'If I have been wrong in my teaching, Father, I am sorry. . . . Forgive me. . . . If this is for today, Lord, fill me with your Spirit!' Whoo! Glory! I felt the presence of the Lord!" The Holy Spirit began to work and move in that local body from that day on. People were healed, and lives were changed. The church went from half full to overflowing. It grew to a point where a second service had to be added. Joe and Sue were happy to be a part of the move of God going on in that community.

The Right Reverend Doctor said he preferred to be called Brother Mark. At ninety years old, Brother Mark decided it was time to retire. He had personally chosen the current pastor, Steve Ricks. He said, "The Lord dropped the name Steve Ricks in my Spirit! I know he is a little bruised from the last church he pastored, but I believe healing is in the house."

Pastor Steve was the perfect fit. Joe and Sue knew if they had a chance after service, he would be the one to talk with about everything that was going on. As soon as service was over, Pastor Steve made it a point to find Joe and Sue. He pulled them off to the side, "What is going on with Frank?" he asked with genuine concern.

"Why, have you seen or heard from Him?" Sue asked, hoping maybe Frank had turned to Pastor Steve.

"The Lord woke me around 4:45 this morning with a sense of urgency to pray for Frank—that he was in danger! The Lord impressed on my spirit that it was a matter of life and death! Is he okay? What can I do to help?"

Joe explained everything to Pastor Steve, who listened intently and reassured them, "God is in control," and reminded them not to blame themselves. The three of them prayed and agreed to stand firm on God's Word.

"Pastor, if it's okay . . . if he hasn't come back by this afternoon," Sue sniffed, "we may come back for the youth service and talk to some of his close friends. . . . maybe he . . . Maybe, he reached out to one of them and mentioned where he might be headed."

Chapter Nineteen
Stacy McInnis

J oe and Sue decided to stay in town, so they went over to Rosie's Place Family Restaurant for lunch. They tried to relax and enjoy lunch. Joe could tell Sue was worried; he could almost read her mind.

"I will call the house after lunch and see if maybe Frank came home while we were at church."

Sue smiled, reached across the table, took his hand, and looked deep into Joe's eyes. "Thank you!"

Though they were concerned, the Holy Spirit was giving them peace and comfort. Joe and Sue were able to relax and enjoy spending time walking around downtown. They found a payphone, so Joe dug in his pocket and found some change. He dialed the home number, and the answering machine picked up.

"Son, Mom and I are hanging around town. If you get this message, we will be home around 7:00 and would like to talk when we get home." Joe paused . . . "love you!"

The youth service started at 5:00 p.m., and Joe and Sue got to church around 4:40 p.m. Their plan was for Sue to talk to Stacy McInnis; she and Frank were in the church nursery together and had grown up together. They had started dating almost two years ago, and Sue wasn't exactly sure where the relationship stood. Frank had withdrawn from conversations with his mom along those lines when school started this year. Joe said he would talk to Bill Jones, Frank's best buddy since elementary school.

Stacy pulled into the parking lot simultaneously as Joe and Sue and parked a few spaces away

"Hello, Stacy. How are you?" Sue asked politely. She liked Stacy but had not spoken to her in several months.

"I am well, Ms. Sue. How are you?" Stacy asked as she hugs Sue.

"Well, all things considered, we are hanging in there."

"Ms. Sue, what's the matter?"

Sue didn't know how to say what was on her heart, so she simply asked Stacy if she had seen or talked to Frank in the past couple of days. She managed to keep her emotions under control. She did not want to worry or upset Stacy.

"No, ma'am. We have not talked since the homecoming dance; we kinda broke up that night." She was still angry and upset with Frank that night, but she was not about to say anything hurtful to add to whatever was going on.

"I'm sorry, Stacy. Sweety, he hasn't been very talkative lately about anything and especially not about his personal life."

Stacy looked Sue in the face, "Is he all right, Ms. Sue?" Even as bad as she had been hurt the night they broke up, Stacy still cared very deeply for Frank.

Sue took extreme care not to let her face betray the flood of emotions she was currently experiencing as she answered, "He left the house mad yesterday afternoon. He said he was 'tired of living under our roof and our rules!'"

Sue sniffled as she felt her bottom lip quiver a bit; taking a deep breath, she continued. "We thought he might have talked to some of you guys last night, you know, looking for a place to stay."

"No, I'm sorry." Stacy grabbed Sue and gave her another huge hug. "I doubt he would call me, but if he does, I will let you and Mr.

Joe know." Stacy's mind was racing, and her heart was filled with emotions that she did not dare show.

"Thank you, Stacy."

Sue had a random thought of how she would love to have Stacy for a daughter-in-law.

Where did that come from? Sue thought with a hopeful smile.

"Ms. Sue!" Stacy turned back as another thought hit her, "You may want to talk to Bill; he should be here tonight. You may also want to ask Toby Nichols," the thought of Toby made Stacy queasy, "He and Frank have been hanging out a good bit."

Sue looked around and realized Joe had walked inside. He more than likely went to talk to Bill. She thanked Stacy for her help and made her way toward the door; grabbing a Kleenex from her purse, she quickly dabbed under each eye and swiped under her nose. When she walked through the lobby, Sue found Joe had taken a seat toward the back. Youth service would be starting in less than five minutes, so she whispered to Joe that Stacy had not heard from Frank.

"Did you know they broke up?"

Joe tilted his head to the right and gave a quick "no" head shake. Joe did his best to whisper that a few seconds earlier, he had seen Bill come in another door and would make sure to catch him after service.

When the service started, Joe and Sue were glad they sat toward the back. They knew the words to the praise songs, but they were not used to them being played that fast and definitely not that *loud!* Then, as the music softened, the band led everyone into a time of worship. The Holy Spirit fell in the place. With the power of the Holy Spirit in the service, no one thought twice about the tears streaming down Stacy's cheeks.

The tears were a result of Stacy remembering her last evening with Frank. Stacy and Frank had grown up in the church together. Stacy could not remember a time-when she did not know Frank. She also had a crush on Frank as far back as she could remember. Stacy even remembered telling her mom in elementary school, "When I get big, I'm marrying Frankie!" Of course, she was only eight, and much had changed since grade school. The summer before their junior year started, Frank finally asked her out on an actual date. They had done many things with the youth group from church, but never on a real boy/girl date. He was the star football player, and she was a cheer-leader, so their dating seemed only natural in the realm of high school teenagers. Frank always treated her with the utmost respect, like a lady. Things started to change when school began their senior year.

She remembered, *It slowly started to slip away after Mr. Stone died, and Frank chose to start hanging around with Toby Nichols* (She shuddered at the thought.).

Frank would plead, "Come on, Toby is having a kickin' party, and we are like the most popular couple in school, so we need to show up at least. We'll just go for a little while; let people see us and stuff."

Stacy's answer was always the same, "No way! Can't we go do something else?" She had heard stories about those parties: alcohol, drugs, sex, and she had no desire to be anywhere around them. Several girls had warned her not to go near Toby or his parties. "That was the biggest mistake. . . ." She had heard more than one girl at school say. A couple of girls even said they thought they had been drugged and taken advantage of while there. Not only was it the pres-sure to go to the parties, but also the pressure to have sex.

"Come on, Stacy. I'm ready to take our relationship to the next level! All the couples are doing it. I love you, and if you love me, then you need to show me!"

The final straw in Stacy's book occurred the night of homecom-ing. The football team had beaten their district rival, 38-0. After the game, Frank and Stacy each cleaned up and changed out of their uniforms, then headed to the Lions Club for the homecoming dance. The dance was a casual event with snacks, dancing, and fun times. Saturday night would be the formal banquet with a sit-down dinner, pictures, and the crowning of the king and queen, which, of course, everyone was saying would be she and Frank. They met in the parking lot around ten-thirty and walked in together. Homecoming started to head in the wrong direction for Stacy when she could smell alcohol on Frank's breath.

"Have you been drinking again? You promised you would stop."

"Relax, I only had a beer with the boys after the game."

"You promise?"

"I promise." Frank thought about the beer and the several shots to toast their victory. *Seems childish, but does a promise count if your fingers are crossed?*

Stacy was having a great time with everyone from school, celebrating the victory, dancing and laughing with friends. Frank was ready to take a walk and get a breath of fresh air after only a couple of dances and, even though she did not want to leave the party, she agreed. Still annoyed about Frank's drinking, Stacy thought this would be a good time to talk about everything going on. They walked out of the building and headed off down Main Street.

"Where are we going?" Stacy naively asks, knowing there are no businesses open within walking distance of the Lion's Club.

"Nowhere, in particular, just felt like walking!" Frank gave a quick answer, looking away and avoiding eye contact. He knew where he wanted to end up. They walked a little farther, then quickly rounded a corner.

Wow! This is dark! was Stacy's first thought and a lot spookier at night.

"Don't be afraid; I am here to protect you."

The little imp that had a young boy shoot out the street light with his new BB gun earlier admired his handiwork. Now, his evil spirit brothers could go to work. Frank pulled Stacy close and started kissing her.

"*Mmm!*" Stacy liked that very much.

He started to kiss her neck.

Even better, she thought, as her mind and hormones raced.

In his mind, images from the adult movies Frank had watched at Toby's raced through his head. The demon of lust was forcing images in Frank's head as fast as his brain could process.

"Slow down!" Stacy knew she was dangerously close to a line she was not ready to cross.

Frank whispered, "I want this to be special. I've got protection. . . . and I've got these pills that make everything . . . you know . . . more awesome . . . They are called X, and it makes it, you know . . . better, and all . . ." Frank pressed in and continued to kiss her neck and ear.

"No!" Stacy's mouth said no, but her body was saying, "Oh yes!" Frank's huge arms wrapped her so tight.

"No! Frank, stop!" She could not move. "I mean it, Frank! Stop now!"

The lust demon was shouting in Frank's head, "No really means yes! She really wants to; she just doesn't know it yet."

Fear rushed into Stacy's head as she realized, "He is going to rape me! He is not going to stop until he takes what he wants! Lord, I don't want to lose my virginity this way!"

Frank loosened his grip around her waist and began to paw at the buttons on her jeans. She found herself no longer looking in the eyes of her Frankie but the lust-filled eyes of a huge teenager. At that moment, when he was about to achieve success with the buttons on her Levi's, she cried out, "Jesus, help me, please! This is not what I want!"

The huge angel that had been forced to sit by and watch the events unfold sprang into action faster than the speed of light. He had endured the taunts of Lust long enough. The angel grabbed Stacy's arm just as Frank leaned in to examine the buttons.

"*Pow!*"

Stacy's forearm landed right across the bridge of Frank's nose. The blow sent Lust, Perversion, and the spirit of rape tumbling, wings and claws flailing, crashing over each other, temporarily blinded by the flash of heavenly light unseen by human eyes. The trio shouted vile curses through the coughing and wheezing as they attempted to regain composure. Unheard by human ears, these curses are nothing new to this massive angel of the Lord. As with every encounter with these eternal evil ones, they weren't destroyed, only sent away until the next good versus evil conflict. At least the demonic forces knew better than to try this huge Heavenly Warrior standing before them, sword drawn, ever ready for battle.

"We'll be back!" they hissed, having had their plan to destroy Stacy's life foiled.

The blow was enough to make Frank's eyes water, and more importantly, out of reflex and pain, he let go of Stacy and grabbed his nose. How in the world did a five foot four, 115-pound girl deliver such a blow? He had hit two hundred-plus pound fullbacks that didn't hit that hard. "Stacy, wait! I'm so sorry!"

The voices of the demons in his head were gone, replaced by cobwebs.

"No way, I have to go!" She walked rapidly away. She was not afraid; she was upset with herself for being so naive and putting herself in that position. She prayed as she walked briskly back to her car. "Father, I am sorry, and I will not put myself in that position ever again." Tears streaming down her cheeks, she felt disappointed and hurt, betrayed by the boy she loved, the one she's had a crush on as long as she could remember, the one she thought she would marry. Frank was ready and willing to cross that moral line—even if by force. How could he? He knew how she felt about sex before marriage, but he did not care; he was not going to stop until he got what he wanted. The thing that hurt her heart and scared her most is that, for a split second, she did not want to stop either. She was thankful they had met at the dance and she had her own ride home. She hated the thought of having to find a ride, or even worse, having to call her dad to come and get her, which would lead to a thousand and one questions she did not want to answer. She flung the car door open and slid behind the wheel. *Bam!* She slammed the door. *Click.* She locks the door out of habit. *Thud!* Her head hits the steering wheel. "Okay, Lord . . ." Her mind racing in every direction, she felt the need to pray but was unsure of what to pray.

Click, click, tap, tap, tap.

"What the heck?" Stacy sat back, slightly startled.

Frank tried the door and found it locked, so he lightly tapped the glass with his knuckle.

She rolled down the window about an inch. "*What,* Frank?" she asked, totally irritated.

"Come on, Stacey. Open the door, and let's talk. I said I was sorry! Please, I love you!"

He stood with his hands on his knees and a puppy dog look on his face. She thought to herself, *He looks so sad.* Before she could think any further, "No, Frank!" she popped before she can second guess.

"What time do I need to pick you up for the banquet tomorrow?"

She looked at Frank's nose, which was looking a little puffy, then to her left index finger that bore his class ring.

"No, Frank, not tomorrow! No homecoming banquet for us!" She slid the ring off and dropped it through the gap in the window.

Frank reached forward and bobbled the ring but still made the catch before it hit the ground. As much as it hurt her heart and as much as she wanted to be Homecoming Queen, Stacy knew this was the right thing to do. She started the car and drove off, leaving Frank standing in the parking lot, looking confused in a cloud of dust, eyes bouncing between the ring in his palm and the fading tail lights on the car driven by the girl who loved him more than he could ever imagine.

Stacy sat quietly as Brother Bobby preached the youth service, not hearing much of what he said but remembered everything from her last date with Frank. She remembered the evil she had seen in his eyes. She remembered every single emotion she felt that night. Then she remembered the peace she felt that night on the drive home. The Holy Spirit reassured her that God was in control and everything would be all right. She prayed in her head, "Lord, I know right now Frank is on the road that leads to destruction. Lord, please watch over him, and help Frank get back on the right path." As much as she loved Frank, she knew they couldn't have a relationship until Frank's heart was right.

"Amen." Brother Bobby had finished his message, and everyone stood to sing the last song. Someone passed Stacy a tissue box. She accepted, dried her eyes, and stood, joining the rest of the singers. After service, Stacy noticed Frank's parents had caught up with Bill. No way could she ever tell them what happened; she could never tell anyone. In her heart, she still loved the Frankie she had grown up with, but she never wanted to see the evil she had seen in those eyes again.

Chapter Twenty
Billy Jones

Billy Jones had known Frank and his family since elementary school. The Jones' had moved to town when Billy was in the second grade. It was tough at first for Billy, being the new kid in a school where everyone else had known each other their whole life.

"You can't play on this swing. You can't play on the see-saw either. . . . We don't allow new kids. . . . You gotta pay us to play on our playground!" A couple of fourth graders decided to make life difficult for Billy.

Billy was not overly happy having to move 1500 miles away from his old school and friends. He just wanted to make the best of the situation and fit in. After several days of verbal abuse, Billy had taken all he could handle. He was tired of sitting on the steps at recess and watching everyone else play and have fun. Billy got up to play, and the bullies started their taunts. Frank, who was in the second grade, was bigger than most of the fourth graders. He walked over and attempted to help Billy. "Leave the new kid alone!"

"It's okay; I got this!" Billy looked at Frank with a snaggletooth grin and a look of mischievousness in his eye.

"Oh, you got it all right."

The bigger of the two bullies laughed and pushed Billy with both hands to the chest. Billy staggered back and rebounded like a wrestler off the ropes and pushed the bully back. The bully sprang forward, intending to push Billy down this time. He soon discovered his target was not there. Billy sidestepped the advancing bully and stuck his leg out, tripping him. Billy jumped on his back with both knees as momentum carried the bully to the ground and knocked the breath out of him. Billy put his forearm on the still-struggling bully's neck to catch his breath and whispered in his ear, "I can play anywhere I want to play!"

After that, Billy had no trouble fitting in with his classmates, and he and Frank became best friends. Frank invited Billy to church, and he and his family became regular members soon after. Along the way, Billy dropped the *"y"* and became Bill.

Joe gave Bill a brief rundown of what happened the day before. "No, sir, I haven't talked to Frank since before Mr. Stone's funeral. He kinda started hanging out with Toby Nichols after Mr. Stone died. It's like Frankie . . . I don't know, Mr. Joe. . . ."

The last time he had invited Frank to youth Bible study, he thought, *Frank is mad at God.* Bill could remember the rage he saw in Frank's eyes. *He blames God for Mr. Stone dying.* That pretty much summed it up, but no way could he say that out loud; he couldn't believe the thought even entered his mind about his best friend. He had not even considered the fact that the guy that first invited him to church had turned his back on anything to do with church and God.

"You know, Toby's into cars and motorcycles and stuff. Do you know Toby? He would be the one Frank would hang out with if he needed a place to stay. His dad owns Nichols' Motors; you know, the big car dealership, as well as-some other places around town!"

Joe and Sue nodded; they had heard of Mr. Nichols. They finished talking to Bill, "If you hear something, please let us know. Tell your dad we need to plan a fishing trip."

"Yes, sir, Mr. Joe. I will. I know he would enjoy that."

Joe and Sue got in the car to head toward home. Neither of them realized how much time Frank had been spending with his new friend Toby. The way it sounded, Frank had shut out his childhood friends for Toby, the new kid in town. Toby and his dad had only been in town about a year and a half. There was a lot of behind-the-back whispering around town, and none of it was good. Mr. Nichols was very wealthy, well-connected, and powerful. He was not afraid to do whatever it took to get what he wanted. Rumor had it; he conveniently *found* an error in the tax-returns of the previous owner of the car dealership. It was a simple, unintentional error that could have easily been fixed, but Mr. Nichols had applied just the right amount of pressure and got the dealership for a fraction of what it was worth. He also bought a couple of restaurants in the next county that were converted into bars and provided "adult entertainment." People wondered why it suddenly became legal to sell alcohol in a county that had historically been dry. He was also able to expedite the permit procedures for opening that type of establishment. Surely it was a mere coincidence that all the council members were driving new vehicles with Nichols' Motors stickers on the back.

The sheriff had also gotten to know Toby and his father's money. Toby had been stopped on a routine traffic stop, and drugs were found in the trunk. When the arresting officer got to the station with Toby, the county judge had left a message, "Release the young Mr. Nichols, immediately, and apologize for any inconvenience that you may have caused." A few days later, the sheriff's office received a large anonymous donation.

The high school kids said Mr. Nichols often left the house to Toby for days at a time. "Whatever you do, don't get the police called. I have already funded enough law enforcement pension plans." The Nichols' home was known as party central among the kids, and most parents were clueless about what was going on.

Joe told Sue he would ride by Nichols' Motors first thing Monday morning. "I'll stop by and see if Frank is staying there. I don't know this kid Toby, so it would be better for me to talk to his dad."

Sue agreed, "I have heard Mr. Nichols has a short fuse, and he might take offense to you interrogating his son."

"I'm not interrogating anyone; I am just trying to find out if anybody has seen or talked to Frank," Joe answered.

"I know, but sometimes your words and tone of voice don't reflect the intent of your heart. People who don't know you don't realize you're a big ol' teddy bear."

Chapter Twenty-One
Breakfast at the Diner

Frank headed on down I-80; he decided Lexington, Nebraska, would be a good place to stop for gas, breakfast, and a quick look at a map. It would take forty-five minutes to an hour to get there. Hopefully, that would be a nice cushion, should authorities seek him in connection with the early morning events. He could almost hear a local news person uttering those words. Why couldn't they call it what it was? How come the headline couldn't be, "The police would like to congratulate the person or persons who put a butt whipping on two punks in the Fort Kearney State Recreation Area." Frank was amazed at what he found amusing as he headed west toward adventure. He pulled off the interstate and found a gas station/diner. It would be great to take care of everything in one stop.

Frank went in and gave the cashier a ten, "This should cover it."

He filled the Harley up, *Almost five gallons! Must have been running on fumes,* Frank thought to himself. "Even at a buck and a quarter a gallon, that's still not bad. I just have to keep a closer watch on the fuel gauge," Frank thought out loud. He pulled the bike around in front, went in for his change, walked over to the diner, and ordered breakfast.

Frank chose to eat at the counter when he heard the police scanner and C.B. behind the bar. Turns out, the diner owner's husband was a trucker and on the road a lot. She liked to hear what was happening out there.

"So, is there anything interesting going on this morning?" Frank nodded toward the C.B. and asked casually in conversation. He had already learned his waitress/chef was more than willing to share any gossip she knew with anyone who would listen. He now knew all about the regular cook.

"He is probably hungover again. If he weren't such a good cook and my brother-in-law . . ." The waitress went on, "I'd fired him years ago. It is a good thing we are slow on Sundays. Any other day, and well, I can't do it all myself!"

According to Frank's newfound friend, "Some teenagers had let a party get out of hand and trashed a cabin over at Fort Kearney. A few of them were taken to the hospital, some with alcohol poisoning, and a couple that looked like they decided to trade licks with a baseball bat."

It didn't sound to Frank like they were looking for him. He thanked his waitress, "I don't know how good your regular cook is, but I can't imagine he can do any better than this!"

"Aw, honey, if I didn't know better, I'd swear you were flirting with me."

He smiled. She had to be at least ten years older than his mom. "Sugar, if you keep flashing them dimples, I might have to leave this diner and my old man and head out with you!" She laughed a raspy smoker's laugh, "Heck, I don't think my big old butt would fit on the seat of that fancy motorcycle you're ridin'!"

Frank did not know what to say, so he just smiled, blushed a little, and thanked her again. He made sure to leave a nice tip as well.

Frank walked out and looked at the traveler's map hanging on the wall outside. He would stay on I-80 for at least another three hours before he hit I-76 toward Denver. Vegas would be at least a two-day ride and five or six more stops for fuel. Six to seven hours of riding a day were more than enough for his backside to endure. Frank planned to stop around I-76 for fuel and rest. Then he'd head toward Denver and maybe find a cheap motel for the night. Frank did not know if he could stand the excitement of sleeping under the stars a second night. It would also be slightly cooler in Denver at night.

Frank put on his helmet, turned the key, and started to kick the Harley's kick-starter when his waitress friend walked out. The surprise must have shown in his face as she burst out laughing.

"Relax, Sweetie. I ain't planning on going with you; I just stepped out to smoke!" She laughed again and blew him a kiss as she tucked the tip money in her bra.

Frank chuckled back as he thought, *It should be safe in there.*

"Be safe, sugar!" she called, as he gave the Harley a kick.

"Yes, ma'am!" he called back and waved as he rode off toward the interstate. During their brief time together, Frank and his waitress had managed to make each other's day. Frank smiled as another traveler pulled into the diner. "You have no idea what's in store for you, Buddy!"

He accelerated and let the V-twin make a little noise. Frank hit the interstate and continued on his journey westward. He would be hitting the Colorado state line about the time he needed to stop again. He ran into spots of heavy traffic but nothing to cause any major issues. Frank found himself more able to relax. He didn't feel as pressed to put distance between himself and his parents or the police. Frank had gone over the plan several times in his head. He liked it more and more each time he replayed it. He would ride about two and a half hours or about 130 to 150 miles, then stop for fuel, stretch, and take care of any other business. It would not be any problem to make it to Denver before dark. He could find a cheap motel, get a good night's rest, and tomorrow night be in Vegas.

Chapter Twenty-Two
Welcome to Denver, Meet Tiny!

Everything was going according to plan. After a fuel stop to top off the tank in Denver, Frank began to look for a cheap place to stay, indoors this time. Something didn't feel right, the Harley wasn't running right, and it wouldn't idle right whenever he had to stop at a red light. He noticed a shop with several nice cars and bikes outside, and the doors rolled up. He thought it odd that a shop would be open on Sunday afternoon, but he wasn't complaining. Hopefully, it would not be a serious problem, but if it were, the shop would likely have what he needed. He pulled in and burped the throttle. Before he could step off the bike, several rough-looking, very large gentlemen stepped out of the shop.

I just made a huge mistake! Frank thought.

They formed a circle around Frank. *Were they sizing him up or checking out his Harley? Well, they wouldn't take it without a fight.* A million thoughts flooded through Frank's head, the main one being, *I am going to die.*

Then a grizzly bear in a mechanic's shirt spoke, "I'm Tiny. How can I help you?"

Before he could think, Frank blurted, "Sir, you are anything but Tiny."

Everybody laughed, which didn't make Frank feel any more at ease. Tiny was at least six inches taller and over a hundred pounds heavier than Frank. All of the other gentlemen appeared to be very healthy and rough as well. Frank proceeded to explain what his bike was doing. As he was finishing, Tiny asked, "Where you from?"

"I'm from Iowa, sir!" Everyone but Frank laughed again.

Another one of the human giants spoke, "I-O-W-A, idiots out walking around, right?"

Frank felt his blood start to boil as they all had another good laugh at his expense.

"Relax, fellow. Nobody here is going to mess with you! Just yanking your chain. We are all brothers here, and brothers help each other out. Did you put this bike together?" Tiny asked, looking much closer at the Harley.

"Yes, sir!" Frank answered with pride. Everyone laughed again.

"Please don't call me sir again!" Tiny responded. "All you need to do is make a carb adjustment. If you are going to be hanging around at these higher altitudes, you may want to change the jets because the air is thinner. This ain't flat, old Iowa anymore! If you are just passing through, a little adjustment is all you need."

The light bulb had come on. Frank could not believe he hadn't thought about that. Mr. Stone would have known immediately.

"What's your name?" one of the guys asked.

"Frank, Frank Carter, but everybody calls me Tank."

Well, Mom is hardly everybody, but he needed a tough nickname for the road, Frank thought to himself.

"Hey, Tank, you need some tools?"

"No, I'm good!" Frank raised the edge of the seat, revealing the custom tool bag Mr. Stone had built. Frank's new buddies were impressed with the workmanship in his bike.

"Man, where you headed from here?" one of the guys asked.

"Vegas," Frank answered in a hurry.

Able to sense that was a sensitive area, another guy asked, "Dude, did you shoot that black lacquer? That is slick, bro. That has to be at least ten coats, and all hand-rubbed too."

"No, a good friend laid it down for me." Frank answered with a smile, remembering the hours he and Mr. Stone had spent on the Harley.

"Man, whatchu think he would charge me to lay some color on my old Indian?"

"Sorry, man. No can do; he's gone. Cancer took him." Frank's smile was gone at the thought of how much he missed his old friend.

"Dude, sorry to hear. Cancer is no joke; took my old man when I was a kid!" Tiny said, turning his head to spit as if to spit the taste of cancer out of his mouth. Tiny offered words of encouragement, "Bro, you just gotta stay strong. As Paul said, you got to run the race set before you."

Hold on. Back the truck up. Did this big biker dude just reference the Bible? Frank's mind swirled, *This ain't even funny. The very same religious crap I'm trying to get away from slams me in the face.*

Frank responded to Tiny with a bit of irritation in his voice, "You sound like the preacher back home! What's your deal? Should I call you Reverend Tiny or what?"

The guys laughed. "Reverend Tiny," they repeated.

Frank listened half-heartedly, out of fearful respect, even though his fourth-dimension traveling companions are extremely agitated. He could feel his heartbeat in his chest and temples. Lately, any mention of heavenly things caused the same antsiness in Frank's spirit.

Tiny's face got really serious as he honed in on Frank's wandering eyes. "About five years ago, I was in the streets, running fast and living hard. I was into a little of everything: running women, drinking, selling drugs, you name it, I did it! Anything I could do to hustle a buck and have a good time! Dude, I was wide open on the path. I am afraid you, my friend, are starting down! Then, I crossed paths with a fellow on the streets by the name of Robinson. He told me about Jesus and His love for me. At first, I wanted to punch him in his mouth. It seemed like every time I turned around, there he was. I swear, I thought he was following me! Turns out, he was only following the leadership of the Holy Spirit. I finally listened when I hit bottom, I took three bullets intended for my boss. The boss left me to die in my own blood. One person was there; he saved my life. Dude, it changed my life forever. I experienced the love of my Heavenly Father through a man called Robinson. If you are hell-bent on going to Vegas, you will run into him, I'm sure! Sometimes, you've got to hit bottom before you realize the only place to go is up! Brother, I'm afraid if you go to Vegas, that's where you're headed, the bottom!"

Tiny could sense Frank's agitation, almost as if God Almighty allowed him to look into Frank's very soul for a split second, into the fourth dimension, and see the spirits that were vexing him. He could see the hurt, resentment, rebellion, and anger. Tiny could see the spirit of rage snarling within Frank's spirit man. Immediately, Tiny knew Frank was angry with God, his parents, the church, and anything that represented what he had been taught to be right. Tiny knew this particular demon well; he had fought with him five years earlier, and it had almost destroyed him.

Knowing he was on thin ice, Tiny continued, "I want you to think about a couple of things, then I won't say any more. I was doing time for possession down south in Mississippi, and there was an old preacher man, called Brother John, who quoted some dude. I think his last name was Zacharias, 'Sin will take you farther than you want to go, keep you longer than you want to stay, and cost you more than you want to pay.'"

The burly biker to Frank's right chimed in, "That's good stuff, brother!"

Tiny glanced his way and gave a right-on brother nod, "Second, no matter how far or how fast you run, when you are done running, Jesus will be waiting for you!"

Every one of the bikers said, "Amen." Each of these rough, tough guys had been where Frank was now. Frank shrugged his shoulders. He had heard all of this before, and his spiritual ears were closed.

Tiny convinced Frank to stay at his place for the night. "The couch, she ain't pretty, but she has given rest to many a weary soul!" Home wasn't much: a small two-bedroom, attached behind the shop. Tiny opened the door and shouted, "Add some more water to the soup; we're entertaining a guest!"

"Yes, dear!" Frank could tell by the response it was not the first time Tiny had brought home a guest. Frank soon met the woman behind the pleasant voice emanating from the kitchen. "My name is Victoria; you can call me Mrs. Tiny!"

She really was tiny, maybe five foot tall, with dark hair and eyes. Mrs. Tiny had definite South American features but an almost undetectable Hispanic accent. Over supper, she shared how they had been together through good and bad times and how "God had brought them out of the darkness and into the light." Tiny contributed to the conversation but honored his promise not to preach anymore.

Frank shared vaguely about home, "I'm just taking a little vacation before school starts."

Everyone at the table, including Frank, knew he was lying. He wasn't taking a vacation; he was running from God as fast as his Harley would take him. They talked a while longer, then Frank's host showed him the guest bathroom where he could have a hot shower, unlike the previous day.

"Pile your dirty clothes here, and I will take care of them for you," Mrs. Tiny called out in her almost angelic voice.

Frank got cleaned up and headed for the couch. He found it amazingly comfortable, especially after his previous lodgings. As he lay there, he looked around; this couple didn't have much, but what they had, they willingly shared.

Frank awakened the next morning to the smell of bacon cooking. As he sat up, he heard Mrs. Tiny, "I hope you are not a vegetarian; I made bacon, eggs, and ham."

Frank looked over the back of the couch and saw Tiny looking over the newspaper and sipping a cup of coffee. Tiny said, "Did you sleep all right?"

"Oh, yes! I slept great!" Frank quickly answered. He looked around and noticed his clothes had been washed, folded, and placed in a stack beside his duffle bag. He got up and had breakfast and thanked his host again and again for their hospitality. After breakfast, he went to the bathroom, brushed his teeth, and washed his face. Frank thought it would be a good idea to, in some way, repay the kindness he had received. He pulled out his wallet and placed fifty dollars under the soap dish.

He smiled at himself in the mirror, "Won't that be a surprise?"

Frank gathered up his stuff and packed it away in his bag. He got everything ready, went outside, and strapped it to the back of the Harley. It was still a little chilly out. "Oh yeah, my jacket!" Frank returned to the house, grabbed his jacket, and said a final goodbye.

"If you ever pass this way again or you need us, just call," Tiny said, as he shook Frank's hand, then pulled him in for a bear hug.

"My God, this guy is huge!" ran through Frank's head. He thanked his host once again as he slipped on his jacket and helmet.

"Ride safe," Mrs. Tiny called out as Frank turned the key and gave the Harley a kick. The V-twin roared to life. It sounded much better than it had the afternoon before. Frank eased out of the shop's parking lot and onto the street, headed toward the interstate. He waved back and burped the throttle as he rode off.

"Lord, we ask You to bless that boy and help him find his way back to You!" The couple held hands and prayed together.

Chapter Twenty-Three
Good People, Good Friends

Frank headed west. The plan was still the same; ride two and a half, maybe three hours, then stop for fuel and whatever else. He had filled up less than twenty miles ago, and with the carb adjustment, the Harley was running great. The early Colorado morning was a tad cool, but as the sun made its way toward the midday sky, it was warming up nicely. Frank started this last leg a little later than he wanted, but it had been worth it to make new friends. He pulled in for the first stop of the day around 11:30 a.m. This would be a good multi-task stop. He'd get fuel, food, stretch, and after that huge breakfast, the need for a restroom was ever-increasing. He pulled up next to the pump and went inside to pay. It was starting to warm up, so this would be an excellent time to lose the jacket. As he pulled it off, he noticed something in the inside pocket, an envelope.

A note was scribbled on the outside, "You need it more, Mrs. Tiny."

Inside, he found the money he had left under the soap dish and one of Tiny's business cards for the shop. The card also had a note on the reverse side, "Make sure you finish your race at the right finish line! Call if you need us! Tiny."

How did they know? How did they slip it in his pocket without him knowing? What in the world did that whole race thing mean? Man, they were good people. Frank slipped the money back in his wallet and tucked the card behind one of the picture slots. He knew in his heart that he had made new friends that would help him if he ever got in a bind.

Chapter Twenty-Four
Meet Mr. Nichols

Monday morning, Joe got up early as usual and got ready to head into town. He needed to go to the Co-op, pick up some fence posts and wire, and other things for projects around the farm. He figured he would take care of his other business in town first, then head over to Nichols' Motors and talk to Toby's dad. His reasoning was twofold: first, he didn't think Mr. Nichols would be in until mid-morning, and second, he really didn't want to deal with him. Joe had heard the same stories and more that Sue had mentioned. Mr. Nichols sounded like the type of person he remembered his dad being.

Joe finished all of his other errands and headed over to Nichols' Motors. "Lord, I pray for Your favor in this meeting! I bind off all attacks of the enemy and ask for a hedge of protection around me! In Jesus' name, I pray!"

Joe thought it wise not to see Mr. Nichols alone. Even though he could not see them, Joe knew the Father would place angels to serve as protection around him. Several giant Heavenly Warriors were dispatched to accompany him into what he knew in his spirit to be unfriendly territory. Joe noticed two salesmen standing out front, puffing away on their cigarettes like a couple of steam engines.

"Hey, man. Let me take this one. I need to sell three more, or the old man is gonna, well, you know, my butt can't take any more chewin'!"

"Go ahead. I'm ready to leave this place anyway!" the second salesman responded as they each put out their nic-stic.

The first salesman was at Joe's truck door before he even came to a stop. "How are you today? Good! Glad to hear it! Welcome to Nichols' Motors! What can we show you today? Are you interested in trading your old truck? Will you need to talk to one of our financing agents?"

The salesman talked so fast, and Joe thought, *He has got to come up for air eventually*. He paused for a split second, "I need to see Mr. Nichols!" Joe blurted while he had the chance.

The salesman took two steps back; from the look on his face, Joe guessed Mr. Nichols did not get many social calls. "Ye-ye-yes, sir! Ssseee Deb, umm Debbie inside!" The salesman seemed to have lost any mastery of the English language he may have once had. Inside, Joe quickly saw Debbie sitting at the receptionist's desk.

"Good morning, sir! Welcome to Nichols' Motors! How may I assist you?"

She is very bubbly, Joe thought, as Debbie greeted him. "Yes, ma'am, I would like to see Mr. Nichols, please."

Debbie's eyes widened as a look of shock came across her face. She recovered quickly, "Just a second. Let me page him and see if he can come out and meet with you."

Joe thought this was all very odd. Though he had been waiting several minutes and said very few words to two people, no one asked him his name or why he needed to see Mr. Nichols.

"Debbie, if it is okay, I would like to meet with Mr. Nichols in private." Joe lowered his voice as if not to broadcast his meeting across the showroom. That brought an even bigger look of surprise to Debbie's face.

"Mr. Nichols, sir . . ." Debbie almost whispered in the phone.

"What is it, Debbie?" a loud, annoyed voice yelled on the other end.

"There, there is a gentleman here, um, he is, um, here to see you, sir."

Joe could hear a stream of profanity flowing from the phone's receiver.

"I'll be out in a minute!"

"Sir, he is um, requesting, um, a private meeting." Debbie stammered to get the words out, still almost whispering.

Another stream of profanity followed, then Joe heard, "Send him in!"

Debbie pointed to a single, huge, wooden door with large, two-way mirrors on each side. Joe walked into the large office; Mr. Nichols sat behind a massive oak desk. The room reeked of alcohol, and Mr. Nichols looked like he had been awake all weekend. He motioned for Joe to have a seat. The whole room felt cold, dark, and oppressive, not just in the physical but also in the spiritual sense. Joe glanced around the room at the *artwork*, feeling as though evil eyes were glaring back from the canvases. It was enough to make the hair on the back of his neck stand on end. Some people may call it modern art, but to Joe, it had a certain demonic quality about it. He felt an eerie feeling that he was in the presence of evil, emanating from one very evil-appearing man behind the large wooden desk. The Heavenly Warriors formed a tight circle around Joe, swords drawn and ready for battle. Joe could sense the evil, but his heavenly protectors could see every glaring eye of every vile creature. Evil darted around the room. The protectors stayed on alert as the sound of leathery wings cut through the sulfuric fog filling the air, along with the vulgar taunts of the unholy ones.

"You're in over your holy little heads; this is our human!" a large ancient evil one bellowed.

"Permission to engage these hideous slime balls, sir!" an enormous member of the Heavenly Host pleaded with his squad leader.

This battle veteran kept a hand on the hilt of the sword and eyes fixed on the largest of the dark creatures.

"Negative, we are here only as a protection detail! Hold your position! "the commander scanned the room, prepared for any move against the human in his charge.

It was evident that Mr. Nichols did not have many human guests in his office. As he sat down, Joe said a quick prayer in his head again, "Lord, I really need Your hedge of protection all around me!"

Over each of Joe's shoulders, the two most enormous angels stood with shields, ready for any enemy attack. "No weapon formed against him shall prosper!" the angel over Joe's shoulder served notice to all of the dark spirits in the room.

Joe still only sensed the presence of evil, but the Heavenly Hosts remained ever on guard. Sickness hurled a queasy stomach toward Joe, blocked by a quick angelic elbow. The ever-increasing light of heavenly swords continued to illuminate the spiritual darkness of the room. Mr. Nichols wasn't sure why, but he knew there was something about this stranger he did not like. Actually, the evil in and around him had been at war with those dwelling in and around Joe for centuries.

"Who are you? What can I do for you?" he snapped, and an antagonizing spirit fired off a fiery dart, which the Heavenly Warrior flicked away with a stroke of his sword.

Joe's plan was to take care of this matter as quickly as possible without conflict. "Name's Joe Carter; my boy, Frank, is friends with your son, Toby." Joe began.

"Yeah, so my boy has lots of friends."

The spirits surrounding Mr. Nichols were doing all they could using his sharp tones in an attempt to slice open a spiritual door for their comrade Anger to sink his talons into Joe. They knew if they could lure Joe through the open door and replace his peace with anger, they would have the victory. Fear and Intimidation also began to hover around until the Holy Spirit rose within Joe, providing peace and unexplainable calm. One of the angels standing at attention to Joe's right made a quick swipe with the hilt of his sword and sent Fear and Intimidation sprawling across the room.

"No fair!" the evil duo screamed.

Joe eased to the edge of his chair and, in the natural, spoke in a very calm voice, "I wanted to see if Frank had been by your place in the last couple of days." While it was calm in the natural, the Holy Spirit flooded the spiritual realm, sending demons fleeing to the dark corners as far as they could retreat.

Mr. Nichols calmly answered, "I have been in and out of the house all weekend, you know, business and stuff, but if your boy is the one I'm thinking about, he hasn't been around since, maybe Friday." Now, Mr. Nichols was the one uncomfortable, desiring to end this encounter. "Frank, he is the big boy that rides the nice Harley, right?"

Joe answered, "Yes, sir. That's him."

"Then, no, I am sure I haven't seen him or his bike since Friday."

In his spirit, Joe knew Mr. Nichols had been honest with him and hadn't seen Frank. He also knew he had worn out his welcome, and it was time to go. The demons were beginning to creep back from their hiding spots, and Mr. Nichols was starting to act agitated again.

"Thank you, Mr. Nichols."

"Whatever! Don't let the door hit you on the way out!"

Joe calmly strolled across the dealership; all eyes were on him. Everyone in the room had been in the *back office* with Mr. Nichols at one time or another. When the boss was on the showroom floor with a customer, Mr. Nichols could be as nice as anyone. However, it was a different story when he was in his office or taking care of his "other business." Usually, people emerged with a look of fear or shame after a meeting in the back office. Yet, there was Joe, walking out with a confident smile on his face. All the employees were amazed and confused.

"Thank you, Debbie." Joe nodded and smiled at the still-shaken receptionist. "Good day, gentlemen!" he spoke to the same cigarette-smoking salesmen, still hovering around the ashtray. They also had a look of shock as Joe walked out with a smile on his face. Joe was relieved that even though he did not know where Frank was, he knew he wasn't hanging out with the Nichols family.

Chapter Twenty-Five
When I Was a Boy

As Joe started to head home, memories of his childhood filtered through his mind. Mr. Nichols had reminded him of his father, except this was different. He had not been afraid of Mr. Nichols like he had been of his own father. The most striking memories of his dad were bad, but his mom told him his dad had not always been that way. Joe's mom was the only daughter of a wealthy Texas couple. His grandfather had made his fortune in oil before World War II. He had purchased thousands of acres of land, including the land Joe and Sue now owned. They raised their daughter, Betty, in a Christian home. After the war, Joe's dad came into the picture. Joe's mom was sixteen when his dad came along and swept her off her feet. He was over twice her age, and Joe's grandparents had their reservations.

"There is just something about that fellow that makes me not trust him!" they agreed, both unaware they were dealing with a smooth-talking con man.

Joe's dad had everyone fooled. They were married before Betty's seventeenth birthday, and the newlyweds set off to make their fortune. Of course, Joe's grandparents had given them "a little something to help them get started." Baby Joe showed up before their first anniversary. According to Betty, the first couple of years weren't too bad. Tension started to rise after some bad investments, and with a baby to take care of, the couple found themselves in debt way over their head. Joe's dad began to drink, and he tried to make ends meet by gambling with people you really didn't want to owe money. Anytime Betty mentioned getting help from her parents, Joe's dad would fly into a rage, often showing her the back of his hand in an up-close and personal way.

"I am the man here! I can take care of my house; I don't need any stinkin' charity from your parents!"

Joe could remember the smell of liquor on his dad, and even today, in the office, that stale beer smell made his stomach turn. Joe's memories of getting slapped around for the smallest things came flooding through his mind. When he was about seven, he remembered feeling like he was getting beat to death for "walking too loud."

"Suck it up, boy! Quit that crying! I'm gonna make a man out of you yet, by God!"

Most of all, he could remember the look of hatred in his father's eyes. He had seen that look in Mr. Nichols' eyes. It was a piercing look of hatred as though his eyes were boring a hole right through you. Joe did the best he could to stay away from his dad, especially when his dad had been drinking. His dad had moved them well away from town into an old, dilapidated farmhouse with a leaky tin roof and cracks around the windows. It struck Joe as odd—the memories that his visit to Nichols' Motors had stirred. He allowed his mind to drift back to things he had long ago pushed to the very back recesses of his mind. He remembered how anytime his dad would go away "on business," he would take the only car and take the mouthpiece out of the old black rotary phone in the hall. He would leave them without a way to call for help or an escape from this hell on earth. That was okay because Joe remembered he and his mom were always grateful to get a break when his dad went away. Joe remembered his dad reading all the letters his mom would write home. If she tried to sneak in any information about how they were living, Joe's dad would sit her in the corner like a punished child. He would tear the letter into small pieces and make them into spit wads. Then he would spit them at her and laugh like a crazy person. Yep, his dad had made him the man he was today! Joe knew exactly the type of husband and father he never wanted to become. He only wished he would have been big enough to beat his dad up and rescue his mom from the humiliation she endured. The story was always the same; any interference on Joe's part would be met with the back of his dad's hand. Joe struggled with the feeling of hopeless desperation he had felt as a child. Escaping their home seemed an impossible thing at the time. One saving grace was that Joe could still remember the peace and calm he felt as his mom read to him from the old Bible she kept hidden in the bottom of her old hope chest. It was their inside joke that their only "Hope was in the hope chest!"

In a final act of desperation, Joe's dad found a man willing to loan him money. Joe still remembered the day when the creepy men came to the house and brought the money. He had hidden in the pantry, one of his usual hiding spots, and watched as three men came in to see his dad. The first guy, the one that did all the talking, was short and round. He smoked a nasty-smelling cigar. He didn't use an ashtray; he just flicked his ashes on the kitchen floor. Joe knew he did not like this guy. *Why was he even in our house?*

Joe did not dare make a sound. He was scared of his dad, but these other two men were tall and broad at the shoulders and skinny at the waist. Fear had frozen him in place. Joe could remember getting a good look at one of the big guy's faces. It had several scars where it looked like he had been cut. These two were just plain scary. Either one could crush him like a bug under one of those shiny, black leather shoes. As Joe made the final turn for the last few miles home, he laughed to himself. "They would have been perfectly cast in a gangster movie."

All three wore solid black expensive suits and drove a long shiny black car with big round fenders. There was the overwhelming smell of tobacco and way too much aftershave. Joe remembered the round guy saying, "You just pay when ya s'pose to, ya see, or these two are gonna come see ya, and it ain't gonna be nice! Understand?"

Dad nodded and said, "Yes, sir. I understand. I will have it all!"

A couple of weeks later, the two big guys came back. Joe could hear the dad he feared begging for more time, and this time, Dad sounded afraid.

"Let me check with da boss, and we'll let you know!"

Crash!

The answer came in the middle of the night! Joe hopped out of bed and ran to the hall. He ran into Betty, who was running to check on him. His dad had run to the living room, where they heard the crash.

"What is it?" Betty screamed, as she and Joe made their way cautiously to the living room.

"Two days!" His dad swore as he unwrapped the note attached to the rock that had crashed through the plate glass window in the living room.

"*Bomp! Bomp!*" came the sound of a car horn. The trio looked out to see the long black car pulling down the driveway. The car was in no hurry; they wanted Joe's dad to know who had delivered the message, "Two days!" Dad knew what it meant. Betty brought Joe to bed, tucked him in, and said a quick prayer. She left quietly and closed the door. Joe could not hear all they were saying, but he could hear a lot of yelling and Mom crying. Joe could remember Betty reading, "What time I am afraid, I will trust thee" (Psalm 56:3, KJV). He repeated these four words over and over. "I trust you, Jesus! I trust you, Jesus! I trust you, Jesus!" Joe fell quickly asleep, unaware of the enormous angelic being standing as a watchful guard at the foot of his bed. Outside the farmhouse, shoulder to shoulder, ever-ready for battle, stood a legion of Heavenly Host, fully prepared to defend those placed in their charge. The angels may have been unseen by human eyes, but they were recognized as they stood, swords drawn, by all who may have sought to harm Joe or Betty.

The next morning, when Joe woke up, Betty had cleaned up the glass, and Dad's car was absent from the driveway. Betty knelt down and wrapped her arms around Joe, and squeezed tightly. Her prayer, "Lord, deliver us from evil!"

Betty sent Joe to get dressed. "Go quickly, and I'll have your breakfast ready."

He did not know why at the time; he just knew there was a sense of urgency, and it was a good thing. Joe rushed and got dressed, and when he got back to the kitchen table, Mom had an egg sandwich waiting.

"*Squeeeeek!*" came the sound of brakes from a car in the driveway. Joe's eyes widened in fear. "*Knock! Knock!*" came a light tap from the front door. "*Whew!*" Joe sighed, Dad wouldn't knock, and he did not think the two big guys in black would have knocked politely either. Mom looked relieved as well. Betty opened the door slowly.

"Hello, Ms. Betty!" It was Mr. Jones, the nice old guy from the drugstore in town, and Mrs. Jones was with him.

"Well, hello. What a surprise to see you," Betty said, with a genuine tone of surprise in her voice. They had never welcomed guests before.

"Ms. Betty, we hate to bother you, but could we trouble you for a little water. You see, for some odd reason, Mrs. Jones wanted to take a ride in the country this morning. Well, you know we don't usually drive out this far. You know, on account of we are kinda getting on up in years. Anyway, our old Ford is kinda getting on up in years too. Well, that old radiator is overheating, and if you could spare a spot of water, we would greatly appreciate it."

"Certainly, Mr. Jones. It would be my pleasure; we have a bucket hanging right over here."

Betty rounded the corner and looked to the nail that usually held the bucket. No bucket. There it is, setting fifteen feet away. Betty walked to pick it up. It was already full. As she bent to pick it up, the angel of the Lord spoke into her spirit, "Now is the time! It is time for you to leave."

She looked around, nobody! She started back with the bucket and the angel repeated, "Now is the time! It is time for you to leave." Still, nobody was close enough to have said anything.

Betty got back to where the Joneses were waiting. "Mr. Jones, could we trouble you for a ride to the bus station?" Had those words actually just come out of Betty's mouth?

"Why sure! We would be happy to return your kindness!" Mrs. Jones spoke up while Mr. Jones loosened the radiator cap.

"Odd, barely even warm, not even hardly low on water!" Mr. Jones scratched his head as he thought out loud.

"I'll just be a minute," Betty called out, as she sent Joe out to the old Ford. She grabbed the suitcase Holy Spirit had prompted her to pack earlier. She remembered the secret stash of money she had mysteriously stumbled upon earlier as well. In less than five minutes, she and Joe were in the backseat of the old Ford, headed toward town. Everything had fallen into place with a little help from unseen hands. In the Jones' eyes, it looked like one great big coincidence. Betty knew it was more.

"Thank you, Jesus!" she whispered as she squeezed Joe's hand.

"Where are you headed?" Mrs. Jones asks over the back seat.

"We are headed to Texas to see my parents," Betty answered politely.

Everyone was at ease, even the big angel riding on the hood of the old Ford. He was glad he didn't have to block the wind and make the radiator overheat again.

Joe and Betty hopped on a bus and headed to Texas. A few days later, a couple of police officers showed up at Joe's grandparents' home. They needed to ask a few questions. Joe's dad had been found "beaten to death in front of their burned-out home."

The police said, "We have a couple of suspects in custody. We just need a little more info to tie them to your husband."

Betty and Joe both described the three men that had come to pay them a visit. The police said their description matched the suspects they had arrested. "If we have any more questions, may we contact you?"

"Yes! Yes! Of course!" Betty answered.

Betty never remarried, and she and Joe stayed in Texas, close to her parents, until he and Sue had married and moved to Iowa.

Joe pulled into the driveway. "Where had the time gone?" Despite a rough childhood, he had grown up in a Christian home and had done his best to raise his own son in a Christian home. "Lord, wherever he is, I know you are more than able to watch over Frank!"

Chapter Twenty-Six
Vegas, Baby

F rank continued to head west on I-70. It was a good seven hours of ride time on 70. He could hardly wait to get to Vegas to party. He started to increase the number of stops but reduce the amount of time he stopped; just the essentials—gas, restroom, snack, and go. He would stop for fuel every time the gauge got below half. He didn't want to chance running out in the mountains, miles from a station. Finally: "I-15, Las Vegas keep left." Frank saw the sign. He stopped at the first gas station he came to on Interstate 15. Frank had just passed through some of the most beautiful interstate roads in America, and had he not been a man on a mission, he would have stopped and enjoyed the view. Right now, however, he had one thing on his mind, getting to Vegas. He started doing the math in his head as he pulled back on Interstate 15.

"About 240 miles to Vegas, at 60 to 70 miles per hour, one more quick fuel stop, we should be in Vegas before 10:00 p.m. We change into another time zone, which means an extra hour to party!"

Frank's mind swirled with excitement. He could not wait to have a beer and find some action. "Stacy may be an old-fashioned girl, but the women here would not have any reservations! This is Vegas! The place to party!" Lust was filling his head with all kinds of ideas.

Frank made his last fuel stop right after seeing a road sign, "Las Vegas, 100 miles."

"Double digits to Vegas, baby! Less than two hours!" His mind continued to race with the possibilities. "Okay, time to think smart for a minute."

Frank used this last stop to come up with a plan. He counted out the money he had left after almost three days on the road. "Roughly seven hundred dollars, not enough to live on for months, but it would do until we can find work." Frank shoved three hundred in his wallet and the rest in the secret slot under the tool tray of the Harley.

Mr. Stone had once told him, "When you're traveling, never keep all your cash in one spot. If you lose your wallet, or somebody steals it, you're not left 'flat busted.'"

Frank hopped on the Harley and headed for Vegas, "Look out, Vegas, here I come!"

He rode until he saw a sign, "Spring Mountain Rd, next exit to S. Vegas Blvd." He was headed for paradise. Frank knew he wasn't going to stay on the Strip tonight, but he had to check it out before he turned in for the evening. "This may be the city that never sleeps. . . . Oh, wait, that's New York. This is Sin City. . . . Either way, I need to rest!"

Frank felt the need to party, but after almost three days on a bike, he needed sleep. "I will make one trip down the Strip; then, I'll find a cheap place to stay off the Strip!"

Frank thought about all the options now he had finally made it to the Strip. He tipped his helmet back so that it rested on the back of his head. Frank couldn't believe the sights and lights. He didn't want to miss a single detail.

Wow! There was Harrah's, and it did look like a giant neon riverboat; it was huge! It had to be almost as long as two football fields.

Frank eased on down the Strip, careful not to run over anyone. He wanted to see all the sights, but he had to watch for cars stopping, people walking, hollering and whistling, and giving thumbs up. "Cool, I think I just saw Elvis. I knew he was alive; there he is again!"

Frank laughed to himself. He felt giddy, like he was on sensory overload. "Check it out, Caesar's Palace and the famous fountain!"

He remembered watching Robbie Knievel jump the fountain that had almost killed his dad, Evel. "No way would he even be tempted to even try it, not for the money, the fame, and especially not on the Harley."

Frank made his way down the Strip and exclaimed, "This is it! I have arrived!" He made his way in front of Bally's. It looked just like in the movie he had just seen starring Robert Redford and Demi Moore. He had to stop to take it all in. Frank eased to the side of the road, his mind wandered, and Lust started to play in his mind.

"Demi Moore and one million dollars, indecent or not, he would make that proposal in a heartbeat."

Frank sat on the Harley, right arm by his side, letting the Harley idle. He must have zoned out for a minute. A leather high-heeled boot passed in front of his face. It truly caught Frank off guard. The Harley, Frank, and the long-legged redhead, now straddling the tank, almost fell over.

How in the heck did she do that? His mind raced in different directions. "What are you doing?" was the first thing out of Frank's mouth as he looked into two of the greenest emerald pools called eyes he had ever seen.

"Let's go for a ride, big boy."

Frank's new passenger wrapped her ivory porcelain arms around his neck as she leaned in with her ruby red lips, close enough for Frank to feel her warm breath on his cheek.

"For a hundred, you can take me for a 'ride'!"

Her voice was so soft and sexy Frank found it extremely difficult to concentrate with his new friend on board. She may not be Demi, but with her fiery red hair, lily-white skin, deep green eyes at five foot eight inches tall, she was all woman! The fact that she wore a denim mini-thigh skirt with legs that went all the way to the ground did not hurt either. It was truly lust at first sight for young Frank, and then from his own lips, he said, "No."

Where did that come from? They were both shocked by Frank's response.

"No?" she repeated. "What do you mean, no?"

Her tone was not as sweet or even close to being as sexy as before.

"Um, no thanks?" Frank responded like a schoolboy, not so sure about his answer in class.

"Why did you stop here if you're not looking for a good time? she asked, almost with a sound of hurt.

"I'm sorry, a misunderstanding!" Frank stammered around, tripping over his words.

She stepped off, not quite as graceful as she had stepped on Frank's bike.

Thonk.

She curled her fist and popped him on top of the helmet, knocking it back down over his eyes. He pulled his helmet off and looked into the eyes of a very hot working girl. She looked about his age, maybe a couple of years older. His mind was racing with every goofball line he had ever heard in every goofy teen movie he had ever seen. She wasn't a high school girl, and he wasn't asking her to the prom. She was a prostitute, and he had just turned her down.

"What a bonehead; you just said no to a hooker!" Lust screamed inside his head. "You haven't been in 'Sin City' fifteen minutes and already rejecting a woman with experience."

"Uhm, excuse me, miss, uhm, could I, uhm, change my answer?"

She was standing on the curb with her hands on her very sexy hips. "Hey, Tex, why don't you tie your horse around the corner and treat a working girl to a 'Midnight Special'?" she asked, with her emerald green eyes fixed on him.

Frank sat dumbfounded and mumbled, "So much for being smooth with the ladies."

"Tex, come on before the cops show up; turn right, and I'll meet you by the lot attendant. Slip him a twenty, and he will watch your stuff. His name is Bobby. He is a friend."

"Okay!" Frank managed to get his mouth to say words. He shifts the Harley to first and eases away from the curb.

Beep, beep!

A speeding taxi gives a warning blast as it zips past. Frank rounds the corner, his bike moving much slower than his brain. "Is she setting us up? Is somebody going to jump us? What's a 'Midnight Special'?" Something in her eyes said she could be trusted.

There was the lot, and Frank saw the attendant stand. Maybe Bobby was her pimp! Frank idled the Harley next to the attendant, and a tall, lanky guy steps out of the shack. Sure enough, he had "Bobby" on his name tag.

Well, there goes the pimp idea! was the first thought. Frank had never actually seen a pimp, other than in the movies, but he could imagine they did not have Bobby's clean-cut un-intimidating look.

"May I help you, sir?" Bobby asked.

Did his voice just crack? I think it did. Frank let out a chuckle, his mind a little more at ease. "A friend of yours said you would watch my bike for twenty bucks."

"A friend of mine? Who? I have lots of friends!" Bobby tilted his head to the side like the RCA mascot.

"Sexy redhead, long legs, emerald green eyes; she's walking around the corner right there." Frank answered with a big smile.

"Veronica," Bobby answered with a sheepish grin.

"Hey, Veronica! How are you? You look real um, pretty tonight!"

"Hi, Bobby. You are so sweet!" The sexy redhead took Bobby's hand and gave him a peck on the cheek, leaving bright red lip prints. Bobby's pale face was now a bright red as he blushed. "Bobby, would you mind if Tex tied his horse in your lot?

Bobby shook his head no and pointed to a spot beside the shack. "No problem." Bobby never took his eyes off Veronica

Frank positioned the Harley in the area Bobby pointed.

"Are you sure it will be okay here?" asked Frank with genuine concern. Bobby held out his right hand and pointed to the palm with his left index finger, never taking his eyes off Veronica. Frank slapped a twenty in his palm, and Bobby responded, eyes still firmly fixed on Veronica, "It will be fine!"

Frank started, "What if . . . ?"

Bobby pointed to two security cameras, "Any trouble and two talking gorillas come out of that door and take care of it."

"Look around, Tex!" Veronica added, with a certain confidence in her voice.

Frank noticed the lot was surrounded on three sides by huge cinderblock walls. The gate he had entered was the only break in a huge wrought-iron fence. The back wall had only two sets of doors, the first, an extremely ornate set of solid oak, at least ten feet tall with the letters "VIP" in elegant gold script. Toward the back corner lay the second set of black metal doors. They too had lettering above, only not an elegant script, but bold block letters, spelling "SECURI-TY." The next thing to catch his attention was how well-lit the area was. This was not a back alley public parking area; it looked like a showroom for limos and exotic cars, cars Frank had only seen in magazines.

"Tex, this is the safest spot on the Strip to park!"

Frank nodded. "There is not a car in here under six figures! What is this place?"

"This, my friend, is where the big money and power in Vegas comes to play. A thief would rather steal from their own mutha than mess with any car in this lot."

Bobby beamed with confidence as he rendered his best tough-guy imitation. Veronica also added a cheesy mob boss imitation, "It's like a magicians convention, ya see. They can make people disappear!"

Bobby and Veronica laughed at her wit and humor. Frank now started to get the full picture, he thought. "So, is it like the Godfather in there or what?"

The two looked at each other and laughed again. "No, not exactly," Veronica began. She looked to Bobby. "Can you explain?"

"Well, you see, it's not like the movies or TV. The mafia doesn't own the big hotels and run the Strip like they used to. Most of the big hotels and casino owners are legit."

Veronica chimed in, "They are big money, and they travel with big muscle; the small ones are probably your size."

"They take pride in their big boy toys," Bobby nodded toward the row of fine automobiles, "these guys would hurt you for standing too close to one of their babies."

"They treat their cars better than their women!" Veronica added. "Now, enough of the history lesson. I'm ready for my 'midnight special'!"

"Good luck, buddy!" Bobby gave a snicker, "You're gonna need it!"

"Thanks, Bobby." Veronica looked back over her shoulder toward Bobby and smirked as she led Frank by the arm back toward the Strip. "So, Tex, I'm Veronica, and since I'm sure you just look like a Tex, what's your name?"

"Oh, uh, I'm Frank. Um, you can, well, you can call me Tank! Yea, that's it! Tank!" Frank's mind was still trying to take in the fact that he is in Vegas, being led toward the Strip, by a hooker, for a "Midnight Special"!

"Um, oh, okay, Frank, I mean, Tank, if um, you're sure that's your name!" she mocked his uneasiness.

"Um, yes, I'm sure it's Tank. That will be fine, Tank!" He continued to trip all over his words.

"Relax, big boy. Don't be afraid. Your friend Veronica will protect you from the mean ol' strip.

He wanted to relax, but one thought kept popping into his head. He could not take it anymore, so he asked, "What's a 'Midnight Special'?" Is that code for some kinda kinky sex or something?"

There, it was out. He said it. Veronica let out a cackle, followed by a snort, followed by a sound similar to human laughter. She laughed, "Can't breathe! Too funny!" and pointed to the sign in front of the Boardwalk. It read, "Midnight Special: All You Can Eat Ribs

$4.99." Frank joined the laughter, more out of relief than humor. "You are buying a *friend* dinner, Mr. Tank, or Frank, or whatever. I may have to go back to Tex if you can't decide what your name is." She continued to laugh at her own humor. Somehow, she did not fit the picture he had in his head of a hooker. Also, he never imagined a night with a prostitute going quite like this.

As they walked toward the "Midnight Special," Frank felt more and more at ease with every step. He couldn't grasp exactly how he felt. In the back of his mind, Lust was throwing all types of images into his thought processes. In the front of his brain, this felt like anything but sexual. He felt like he was just going to hang out with a friend. Veronica had her fingers loosely under his left arm and around his biceps, and her other arm swung carefree by her side, as leisurely as a stroll in the park.

"Why did you call me Tex earlier?" Seemed like as good a place as any, in Frank's mind, to start a conversation.

"Well, you kinda look like a farm boy, to be honest. Besides, not everyone I meet in my line of work uses their real name; you know what I mean? So, was I right? Are you a farm boy? Where you from?" She stopped and looked up at Frank, batting her eyes in mock school-girl infatuation.

He looked down. *She has gorgeous eyes*, he thought. She recognized that teenage boy *ready to get lucky* look in his eye and quickly glanced away, pulling him toward the door of the Boardwalk. "I was raised on a farm. . . ."

"I knew it!" she blurted out. "Sorry, please continue, kind sir!" she giggled.

"Anyway, I was saying, before I was rudely interrupted, I grew up on a farm in Iowa."

"Iowa, you know what that stands for . . . ?" She started.

He finished, "I know: Idiots Out Walking Around!"

"It's all right. I won't hold it against you; I am from Topeka, Kansas." She made sure to raise her voice, almost to a shrill, and drag out the *e* sound in Topeka. "I have been out here almost two years!

120

Hi, Jimmy. I'm sorry, James!" Veronica greeted the cashier. "We'll be having two of the midnight specials!" She giggled again at the thought of the earlier conversation. "Pay the man, Tank! By the way, Sir James of Boardwalk, this is Sir Tex of I-O-W-A, my new friend; also known as Tank or Frank or something like that. Maybe we should keep an eye on him; he seems shady with the whole name thing."

Veronica gave James an over-emphasized wink. James returned the wink with a mock nod of agreement.

"If y'all can wait, about two minutes, I reckon we can wrestle up some hot ribs fer yer eatin' enjoyment." James continued in a very poor southern accent. The trio got a good laugh.

Frank and Veronica had their choice of tables; most of the people on the Strip weren't interested in ribs right now.

"So, what's your story, Tank? What brings you to Vegas? You trying to prove you're a man? You running away in trouble with the law; what's your deal?" Veronica paused from the first round of questioning to take a bite of ribs.

"I just finished high school, supposed to start college in the fall, tired of being treated like a kid, so I left the farm to be my own man; that's my deal in a nutshell!"

"Not bad!"

Frank waved the rib he had just taken a bite of; he had expected shoe leather. "These are actually really good!" Frank wanted to ask the obvious questions bouncin' around in his head but also wanted to be delicate in his approach. The last thing he wanted to do was hurt or offend his new hooker friend. First thought: *How did you become a whore? Nah, maybe more of a joking tone: Was there some sort of an aptitude test that was given in Kansas high schools?* Curiosity was about to get the best of him. How such a genuinely nice girl could be a prostitute was beyond him. So far, all preconceived notions had flown out the window.

"So, how did you, um, end up in Vegas?" he asked, as he took another quick bite from his rib.

"How did I end up in Vegas, or how did I end up a streetwalker in Vegas?" Veronica knew the questions he really wanted to ask, so no need for sugar-coating it.

"Well, yeah! You seem so, well a . . ."

Veronica stopped chewing and focused all of her attention on Frank, enjoying his word tap dance in an almost sadistic manner.

"Normal. I mean, like an ordinary, um, girl, a lady, um, woman."

"Why, Frank. I do declare. I am just as normal as the next girl, Darlin'," responded Veronica with her best Scarlet, southern belle accent.

"I'm sorry. I didn't mean, well, I um, I'm sorry!" Frank's cheeks were now beet red. "It's just; I never knew anyone who supported themselves by selling their body for, you know—sex. How does that work; do you have a license to sell—sex? Do you have to pay income tax? Who decides where you work? Do you rent your corner or what?" The questions were starting to flow. Frank figured since he asked the first question, and she did not pour food or drink over his head, he was safe.

Veronica started the whole laughing and snorting process again, "Hold on a second, big boy! It is time to get a little street education. I guess the best place to begin is the beginning. I do have a *normal job* working as a lunchtime waitress in a restaurant downtown. For some girls turning tricks is all they do. I only do it when the tips are low at the restaurant, and I need rent money or a little extra. Next, contrary to popular belief, prostitution is illegal in Vegas. That's why I didn't want to hang out on the street earlier. The nice casino folks get upset if a bunch of girls start working around their casino. They will call the cops in a hurry. The only place it is legal is at one of the *ranches* or legal brothels, whatever you want to call it. Anyway, I knew a girl who worked out there once; the stories she would tell—not the place for me, no way. Out there, if a client chooses a girl, she does not have much of a say. At least half of the money goes to the house; that's not the life for me. I like to have a say in who I spend my evenings entertaining. I don't have to deal with old perverts. Some girls work for a pimp; this is where the old type mafia comes into the picture. They work some of the clubs and stuff as dancers or whatever, and if a 'client' likes the way she dances, he will work out a deal with her business manager/pimp. Same deal, she has no say, and the pimp takes a cut."

She paused, took a bite, and let everything sink in. "The pimps don't care much for 'independents' like me. We take money from their pockets, so to speak!" She shrugged and took another bite of rib. "I kinda go for the high school/college boy guys, close to my age. It doesn't usually last long; they *tip* well, and they are always in a hurry to leave and go brag to their buddies," she said with a cute, matter-of-fact smile.

Frank could feel his cheeks getting warm yet again. "So, is that why you picked me to take a 'ride'?"

"Yep, sure is," was her speed-of-light response. "Don't worry; you're safe. You are my *friend*, and I don't have sex with friends for money."

Frank's eyebrows went up, and his eyes sparkled with delight. Veronica could tell by the reaction on his face what was on his mind.

"No! It's not free! I don't sleep with friends, period! In this town, it is good to have the right friends. Clients or customers or whatever you want to call them, they just pass through for a brief moment. But a friend will be there when you need them, just 'cause they are your friend."

Ever since she slept with her *childhood friend* when she was fourteen, only to have him tell everyone what a "slut" she was the next day, she had drawn a line in her mind; no emotional attachments with sex. After years of abuse, the one person she trusted with all her secrets had betrayed her. A wall had gone up, and Veronica vowed never to allow anyone to hurt her like that again—ever!

Frank looked down at the plate of bones. James had kept Veronica resupplied. How did that sexy redhead manage to devour that huge plate and never miss a beat in conversation?

"Well, are you done?" he asked with amazement in his voice, as he nodded, drawing her attention to the pile of bones.

Burp! Excuse me!" she responded with a giggle. "Yep, I'm done!"

The two head to the door. "Glad they don't charge by the pound!" Frank chuckled, walking a step behind, friend or not; he couldn't help the thoughts racing through his mind.

"Night, Jimmy; I mean James!"

"Night, Veronica!" James stepped from behind the counter and extended his hand, "Good night, *friend*." He grinned with a knowing smirk and shook Frank's hand. He recognized that *hoping to get lucky* look on Frank's face, but James knew the deal with Veronica and what being her *friend* entailed. They walked back in the direction from whence they came, her fingers around his biceps and her other arm swinging carefree.

"Where are you staying?" she broke the silence.

His mind began racing again. *I would love to spend the night with you!* he thought but did not dare say out loud. "I don't know. Thought I would hang out on the Strip tonight and look for a place and a job tomorrow."

"You can crash at my place if you would like; it is only a couple blocks off the Strip."

His eyes lit up; he might still get lucky.

Smack!

She slapped his arm with her free hand, "On the couch or the *floor!*"

"I know! Golly, gee wiz, Mom," he answered in his best Wally Cleaver voice. Frank knew, but he had hoped for a split second.

Bobby hurried to hide the "adult magazine" he had occupied his time with as the couple approached. "How were the ribs? Did you leave me any?" he laughed.

"Oh, you have seen her eat!" Frank chimed in his response on cue.

"Oh yeah!" Bobby whistled between his teeth, "It ain't nuthin' nice!"

"Okay, you two. Don't make me hurt you!" she said, as she balled up her fist and assumed an old-fashioned boxing stance.

"Well, I hate to be a party pooper, but somebody has to work the breakfast shift in a few hours, and her name is me." Veronica overemphasized a fake yawn.

"All right, let me fetch my trusty steed," Frank replied.

There was the Harley, exactly where he left it. Frank walked the bike around, and they set out to devise a plan to squeeze two bodies and a duffle between the tank and the sissy bar. Frank pushed the duffle bag as tight as he could against the sissy bar and tightened the straps. Frank handed Veronica the helmet and stepped across the bike; a good swift kick and the V-twin roared to life. He nodded, and Veronica stepped across, this time behind him. Frank couldn't help himself, watching the sexy, long-legged, mini-skirt-wearing redhead in the mirror.

"Hey, don't peek, you pervert! Keep your eyes up front!" she said, and she smacked Frank in the back of the head.

Too late, he thought to himself as she settled in between him and the duffle bag. Bobby shook his head and grinned as they pulled up to the street. "Which way home, ma'am?"

Veronica pointed right, "Go to the stop sign, take a left, then the first right. It's the second set of apartments on the right."

They pulled in after about a three-minute cruise. "Do you have a car, or do you walk everywhere?" He could see that it would be less than a ten-minute walk to the Strip.

"Yeah, that's my gray piece of junk parked right there. It doesn't run right now."

Frank could tell it was about a fifteen-year-old Buick with a flat tire. "Maybe I can take a look and help you out, *friend*."

"That would be cool, thank you!"

"Now, look away, no more sneak peeks!" Veronica stepped off, careful not to burn her leg on the hot exhaust of the V-twin. "Pull your bike on that little porch, and bring anything worth anything inside. It ain't exactly the gated lot you have grown accustomed to in Vegas," she giggled.

Frank pulled the bike on the porch, which in all actuality, was more of a stoop. He had to nudge the front tire into the corner so they could get through the apartment door. Stepping off the bike, Frank leaned on the 1950s-style wrought-iron rail, almost falling. He noticed the tie wire holding it in place and shook his head.

"Careful, don't mess up my home!" Veronica shrugged and giggled.

Frank worked himself around the not-so-stable railing and loosened the duffle. He remembered the secret cash stash and unlocked the seat, removing about four hundred dollars. *Got to find a job soon,* he thought to himself.

After about a minute of key shaking and lock jiggling, Veronica gave the door a hip bump, and it sprang open. "Welcome to my humble abode." She placed her left hand on her belly, bowing low, almost in a curtsey, and swept her right hand into the room. Veronica reached for the light switch. *Click.* "Behold, there was light," she laughed again.

While the room was sparsely furnished, Frank was amazed at how tidy everything was compared to the outside. The outside of the apartment complex, as a whole, needed much maintenance. Inside, however, looked freshly painted. The design was simple and efficient. The front door opened into the small living room/dining room/guest bedroom, whatever need arose. Straight ahead, to the right, was an even smaller kitchen in a very liberal sense of the word. Actually, it was more of an indention with a sink, a fridge, and a two-burner cooktop. Straight ahead was the bathroom, with just a very basic sink, toilet, and cast-iron tub. Toward the left corner was a single bedroom, which was basically a room with a bed and not much room for anything else.

"Do you like it? I painted it myself. The landlord deducts a little from the rent whenever I do stuff, but that's not why I do it. You know, this is my house, and I kind of want it to be nice."

Frank nodded in approval.

"So, is that a business expense or does it . . . ?" Frank could tell by the increasing look of hurt on Veronica's face he had started down the wrong road, but it was too late, so he might as well dive in all the way. "You know, is this where you work . . . ? Is that where the action happens?"

Frank gestured toward the bedroom. Lust began to put images in his head. He held up a hundred-dollar bill and made a clicking sound with his tongue and teeth. "Will this cover room and board with benefits?"

"*Jerk*, this is my house! I don't bring clients to my house—I go to a motel—stupid. I only bring friends home, and I thought you were a friend. I told you I don't have sex with, oh, you, get it off your mind! *It ain't happening, not tonight—not ever!*"

Frank knew he had one fired up redhead on his hands and began apologizing profusely.

"You can stay *on the couch* tonight, but tomorrow, you find somewhere else to stay!" Her tone said anger, but her eyes said, "You just hurt me bad!"

"It's okay; you sit. I'll get ready for bed, and then you can get a shower because you *stink!*" Veronica said, as she entered the bathroom and slammed the door.

Frank turned his head and sniffed his pit. "Whew, ripe!"

Behind the closed bathroom door, Veronica wiped the tears from her eyes. She had not let him see her cry, but she knew he had gotten the point. In Veronica's mind, business and personal life had to be separate. She didn't like selling her body, but sometimes, that's why business was business. She had let a stranger into her personal life. *Why couldn't he understand? That is just how it has to be.* Then the lightbulb went off in her head. "Have I got a surprise for you!"

She started the shower and let the hot water run, knowing the water heater would be empty in five or six minutes. Grinning, Veronica remembered she had showered earlier before she went out, so actually, she just needed to remove her makeup, wash her face, and get dressed for bed. She cracked the window where the small room would not retain any heat. "No creature comforts here. A cold shower will do lover boy good."

Veronica let the water run as she removed her makeup. "Now, where was that flannel nightgown, the one grandmother had given me? It should shut down any motor he still has-running. Oh! There it is!"

In the bottom of the linen hamper, still as ugly and unattractive as I remembered. Placing her hand under the stream, Veronica realized that less than a minute of hot water has left. Sticking her head under the shower stream, she rinsed from the scalp to the ends of her hair.

"That should do," she said, and she grabbed a towel. Slipping into the nightgown, she smiled. "No way am I sleeping in this; it's way too hot. I'll change in the bedroom."

Turning off the water, she stepped in front of the sink and brushed her teeth.

"The window." She reached across the tub and shut it. Grabbing the towel, she begins rubbing her hair vigorously, causing it to go in every direction. Glancing in the mirror, she said, "Oh, sexy!" Then she blew her reflection a kiss. As she reached for the door handle, "You look like a mess—perfect!"

Opening the door, she saw Frank still sitting where she left him, with the look of a sad puppy on his face. She almost felt bad for the events she knew would soon transpire. "I am so sorry; I didn't think. I'm such a . . . boy," she finished.

She had started to confess her plot and advise Frank of the cold shower he was about to receive. If he waited ten minutes, the water heater would catch up enough for a hot, quick shower.

"It's okay; we're good. Everything you need should be in the cabinet. Good night. Good luck tomorrow." She went into the bedroom, closed the door, and slipped out of the flannel nightgown and into her long sleep shirt. Into the bed, and thought, *Wait for it. . . .* The joys of paper-thin walls.

Clonk, jeans hit the floor; *squeak* the sound of faucets turning, *thud, thud* the sound of feet in the tub. *Wait for it. . . . Here it comes. . . . five, four, three, yeowh! . . . The sound of cold water meeting a hot boy.*

"Shhhooot! Son of a biiiig, mother of pearl . . ." Frank's voice went up several octaves as the cold water blasted his backside.

Veronica chuckled, "That should cool things off a bit," she whispered toward the bathroom wall, as she adjusted the covers around herself and went to sleep with a smile on her face.

Chapter Twenty-Seven
Day One in Sin City

T he sunlight through the window and the sounds of the neighborhood awakened Frank the next morning. Sitting up, he scanned the apartment for his host, who was not there. Turning to roll off the couch, he shouted, "Ouch! Score couch spring—one, lower back—zero!"

Frank stretched out the kinks; the couch had done quite a number on him. He stumbled the five steps it took to cross the room to his duffle and found a note.

Tank,

I had to work the breakfast shift. Cereal above the fridge, help yourself. Check the milk first; it may have already taken a turn. Let yourself out when you are done. Good luck! See ya around!

Your friend,

Veronica

P.S. I'm sorry about the cold shower. Well, maybe not totally. Sorry. Ha! Ha!

. . .

Frank smiled. "That sneaky little . . ."

He was deeply sorry he had offended his host and would like nothing better than to try and make it up to her. However, he knew she fully expected to come home and find him gone. Frank went to the kitchen and found a bowl. He poured the cereal; he started to pour the milk and remembered the note. Holding the carton under his nose, he took a whiff.

"Close, very close."

It would do for cereal. Frank poured the rest of the carton down the kitchen sink and ran the water. Frank knew he had made a friend that would help him in a bind, but staying another night was not even an option because of his boneheaded move last night. Who could blame a teenage boy for trying to get lucky with a hot, redheaded streetwalker his first night in Sin City? No matter how he tried to justify the previous night in his mind, he knew he had messed up. For some strange reason, Veronica had let him into a special place reserved for a select few in her life. Yep, he had messed up, but Frank swore to himself, "If she ever needs me, I got her back!"

Frank straightened up the couch/spawn from Hell that had him feeling achy all over and washed his breakfast bowl. After brushing his teeth, he got dressed and prepared for a day on the Strip. This was going to be a great day of fun, partying, gambling, and oh, yeah, maybe a little job searching. Frank decided it is time to go, but he should leave a note.

Veronica,

Thanks again for the couch to crash on. Sorry for being a bonehead! You are my first *friend* in Vegas. I owe you one and not for the cold shower. You got me!

Take care. Hope to see you around!

Tank

P.S. Here is $20 for groceries. I kinda ate all the cereal, and the milk was a tad on the bad side.

. . .

Frank gathered his stuff and headed out the door. He decided his first course of action should be to find a place to call home for a few days. The main thing was a place to store his stuff and a place to rest his head, should the need arise. Right now, he felt like he could run for days on the excitement of being in Vegas. Frank knew staying on the Strip was out of his price range. He remembered Veronica said something about cheap motels toward the north end of town but to watch his back in certain areas.

Chapter Twenty-Eight
Welcome to the Lucky Motel

F rank could tell as he moved a few blocks away from the hustle and bustle of the Strip the quality of the nightly accommodations was rapidly declining. A quick check of the finances before leaving Veronica's had revealed two things. First, cheaper was better right now, and second, it was time for positive cash flow. Frank noticed several motels advertising hourly, daily, and weekly rates. The daily rate would be the best option based on current cash or lack thereof. He saw a motel that looked to have been built in the last forty to fifty years with a rate less than forty bucks a night.

"Looks like we have a winner; with a name like Lucky, it had to be a good sign."

The area around did not look too bad, but Frank could tell he was in an older part of town and decided not to wander off the beaten path after dark. The expansion of the Strip had taken a toll on the older sections of town. This area was nothing like the mega hotel/casino strip he had left minutes ago. The motel looked like it had been blasted from 1965 to the present with very few changes. White stucco walls ten years past due for touch-ups and red terracotta roof almost made Frank forget he was in Sin City. The marquee ad for in-room adult movies sparked the interest of Lust, Frank's fourth-dimension traveling companion, who had been strangely silent for the past few hours. Lust bounced around Frank's head, wide awake and ready for action. Frank idled the Harley past the well-worn swimming pool and made his way toward the office.

In the office, Frank met Kandi, the desk clerk, co-owner, and lounge singer. It didn't take long to figure out Kandi had been around as the lounge entertainment for at least as long as Frank had been alive. The first thing he noticed was the "Appearing for Two Shows Nightly" billboard with a picture of Kandi, apparently taken more than a few years earlier. Then his eyes fell upon Kandi, her body not bad for a woman obviously on the other side of forty, with makeup that looked as though she applied it with a paintbrush or maybe even a paint roller.

"Hello," Frank spoke first, drawing her attention away from her game show on TV.

Standing up straight, poking out her chest and in her sexy, soft, raspy, smoker's voice, she said, "Well, hello, stud. What can I do you for?"

Kandi scanned Frank from head to toe.

"Is she flirting and checking me out? Hey, let's play along!" Lust whispers, now ready for anything close to action.

Frank smiled, revealing his dimples and doing his best to avoid turning beet red. "Yes, I would like a room."

"How long do you need it?" she looked past Frank, noticing the Harley and no one with Frank. She leaned over the desk and spoke where only Frank could hear, "I'll give you a break on an hour! I'll show you to the room personally, and I'll show you, well, I'll show you what experience can do for you, big boy!"

Frank leaned close, "How about a rain check?" *What the heck? Where did that come from?* "I need a room for at least a night." Frank maintained his composure and returned to speaking in a normal tone.

"What's your name, and where have you been all my life, big boy?" Kandi asked, still flirting, as she reached for a room key.

"He wasn't even born the first half of your life," came an almost growl from the small office behind the desk.

"Shut up! Bart! Nobody pulled your string!"

Frank didn't understand the mumbling that followed but was pretty sure Bart was not telling him to have a nice day.

"I'm Frank, but you can call me Tank."

Frank tried his best to be smooth. A snort came from the small office, and curiosity got the best of Frank; he had to peek and see the source of the sound effects. There sat Bart, with a sweat-stained wife-beater t-shirt and more hair on his shoulders and back than the top of his head. The hair he did have was slicked back and greased down into a ponytail. He also had several bad tattoos on each arm, exactly like Frank imagined. Twenty years and seventy-five pounds ago, Frank envisioned Bart as a very intimidating sort of fellow. Even now, Frank did not care to be alone in a confined space with this guy, especially if Bart was having a bad day.

Frank pulled out his wallet and quickly paid for one night in cash.

"Bart!" Kandi shouted.

"What?"

"Show this fine young gentleman to lucky room seven!" Kandi said, as she checks Frank again from head to toe with sexy eyes.

Bart swore, ". . . he's a big boy. He can find it!"

"Fine." Kandi swore back. "I'll show him!" She looked into Frank's eyes, blew him a kiss, then licked her lips. Her body language certainly did not match the tone she was using with Bart.

"Good . . . 'bout time you do something besides watch those stupid game shows!"

"Maybe, one day you will get off your butt and do something!" she popped back an answer, never taking her eyes off Frank.

Kinda feels creepy, but I think I might like it. Frank's thoughts were running wild at this time. *Sure, she is at least twice my age, but hey, she still looks hot under the layers of makeup.*

He opened the door for Kandi to lead the way to lucky room seven, and she brushed his shoulder with her hand and made the "Follow me!" motion with her index finger. Like a lamb led to slaughter, Frank followed half a step behind.

"So . . . are you and Bart . . . together . . . like . . . married . . . or whatever?" Frank asked nervously.

"Ha!" she hooted. "Yeah, we are like, together. . . ." She swore. "Like, he's my business partner in the motel and . . . my manager!"

"Manager?" The thoughts began swirling in Frank's head again.

Kandi stopped suddenly, and Frank almost ran into her. "My show business manager! Didn't you see the sign in the lobby?"

"Oh yeah, right. I saw: 'Two Shows Nightly'!" The look on his face must have betrayed his thoughts. *You need a manager to perform in the lounge of a motel you are part owner of?* was the thought on his mind.

"Bart says we are really close to hitting the big time on the Strip, you know, in one of the big casinos. . . . And I might get my own show. . . . and have like, opening acts and stuff!" She said all of that with a twinkle in her eye.

That train left the station ten years ago! was his thought, but Frank responded, trying to be encouraging, "I sure hope that big break is just around the corner!" Frank stepped forward to continue the search for lucky room seven.

"Where are you going? This is it, big boy!"

Frank realized they had walked maybe fifty steps from the office; that's why Bart had been so eager to point the way.

"The last show is at 2:00 a.m. in the lounge. I'll save you a table up front if you like?" Kandi continued to flirt.

"Yeah, sure, that would be awesome!"

"Maybe afterward, I'll give you a personal encore!"

Frank stumbled around with words: "Yes, sure, I'll be, looking forward to it!"

"This is the parking spot for seven." Kandi motioned toward the number seven painted on the curb. "If you could move your bike before Bart complains."

Frank noticed he was parked five slots away from the number seven slot, so he moved the bike before entering lucky room seven.

Unstrapping the duffle, Frank raised the seat of the Harley, finding an old combination lock. He felt good about having a room to leave the bag in while he was the man about town, but he did not exactly trust the top-notch security of the Lucky Motel. The lock would not keep it from being stolen but maybe at least deter someone from messing with his stuff. Inside lucky room seven was no big surprise. It had a double bed, dresser, and nightstand, made out of the finest pressboard circa 1975, complete with cheesy artwork. Everything, including the artwork, had been screwed to the wall to prevent theft. Frank noticed a water stain on the ceiling that had been painted over.

"At least some maintenance had been done in the last four decades."

The linens on the bed appeared to have been changed recently, and he noticed the "Majik Fingers Massage" on the bed.

"What the heck?"

He dug in his pocket and pulled out a couple of quarters. Frank kicked off his shoes and stretched out, feet hanging over about six inches. He was ready to get the most of his five minutes. The process started with a strange hum, followed by a noise similar to a sound he had heard on a documentary about water buffalo. Next, there was movement, slow at first, gradually increasing to vibrate every filling in Frank's mouth lose, then the thought came, *If I hang on for eight seconds, do I win the rodeo?*

After three and a half minutes, Frank could not stand the torture any longer and rolled off the bed feeling a little seasick. A minute or so later, the beast began to power down with the eerie hum of a malfunctioning electric motor. After a quick check for smoke or any other signs of nuclear meltdown, Frank moved on to the nightstand.

It had at least a dozen fliers for everything from erotic shows, adult stores, escort services to pizza delivery with a handwritten note: "No deliveries after dark." He had to check, Yep, there it was, in the bottom drawer—a Gideon's Bible.

Frank quickly checked the bathroom toilet, shower, sink with a dripping faucet and a cracked mirror. It was all there, even a slightly frayed towel. *This sure ain't five stars,* Frank thought, glad he had picked up toiletries. A quick check to the mirror, and he decided to keep the week-old beard.

"Looking a couple of years older may help us get away with some underage drinking later!"

He then noted, "No need to unpack!"

Frank slipped the lock into the eyelets of the duffle and moved it from the floor to the dresser top. All settled in, time to head back to the Strip for some action and some positive cash flow. The plan, since it was still early in the day: hit a few casinos, play a few slots, ask around to see if anyone is hiring summer help.

Chapter Twenty-Nine
Got a Job . . . Almost

Heading back to town, Frank found public parking and decided to cover more ground and see more sights on foot. It didn't take Frank long to learn a few things in his job search. First, to get a job in certain service industries, a person had to belong to the union and carry a union card. Second, when filling out a job application, potential employers didn't take applicants seriously that had the Lucky Motel as an address with no contact phone number. And lastly, most of the jobs he was qualified for had already been filled by local college students.

Then, the idea hit him: *Why not try a construction job?* He remembers seeing The Stratosphere, so he headed over and found the construction office. Inside the small trailer were five guys eating sandwiches and discussing details of the blueprints spread out on the table.

"What can we do for you, son?" asked a fellow wearing a polo shirt and white hard hat, obviously the job supervisor.

"Yes, sir. I need to go to work!"

"What's your trade, boy?" one of the "working men" around the blueprints spoke up.

"Trade?" Frank stammers, not quite sure how to answer.

"Yeah, son. What can you do? What's your skill?" the boss asked.

"I thought maybe a helper or laborer or something."

"Hmmm. Well, son. You see . . ." the boss started.

"Hey, boss. Why not send him to see Red?" one of the other guys said.

Another added, "If he can work for Red 'till five, I say give him a job."

"Now there's an idea! What's your name, kid?"

"Frank, but everybody calls me Tank!"

"Huh? A Tank and a bulldozer, that could be interesting!" The worker with the idea to work for Red chuckled.

"Okay, kid. Go over to the tool room and ask for Red. You'll know him; he is a sawed-off, loudmouth, piece of s--tuff! It is almost 12:30, so he should be back from lunch. If you can make it until 5:00, you got a job at six bucks per hour—cash."

"Yeah, and if you bust him in his loud mouth, well, obviously no job!"

"Now, grab a hard hat from the rack, and good luck. Hope to see you tomorrow!"

"Yes, sir. That sounds like a deal!" Frank shook the boss's hand and thought, *How bad can it be?*

Frank headed over toward the tool room and heard a stream of profanity coming from a short redhead who looked almost as wide as he was tall. Walking up, Frank extended his hand, trying to sound tough, "Name's Tank. I'm looking for Red!"

Red turned and spit, just missing Frank's outstretched hand. "What do you want, bootlicker?"

"The boss sent me to work for you."

"That worthless piece of ——. He is always sending me . . . wet behind the ears . . . young punks!" Red swore, tobacco juice dripping down his chin, "He is your uncle or what? I got a job to run, not a dadgum babysitting service."

Red continued with a five-minute vent on the boss, the job, the younger generation, and some things Frank had no idea how they fit into this shout fest. He was starting to wonder if they called this guy Red because of the hair or the fact that his face turned bright red when he yelled. Apparently, he did the yelling part a lot.

"Don't stand there with your finger in your nose; go get my claw hammer up on twenty. Hurry, snot wad; I got a stinking hotel to build!"

Frank headed toward an elevator sign.

"New guy, where are you going? This is your first day; you have to earn the right to ride my elevator. For now, you can use my stairs."

Frank returned, out of breath, hammer in hand.

"What are you doing, turd? Where is my Skill saw? Hurry up! I got a pallet I need moved!"

Frank returned with a Skill saw, realizing it has only taken a half-hour, and he was ready to bust Red in his loud, foul mouth.

"It's 'bout time; Grandma was slow, but she was old, so I fired her." Red spit, almost hitting Tank again. "Now, get over here and move this pallet of cement from the yard to the shed; looks like rain."

As Frank stepped up on the forklift, he heard Red, "What are you doing, you dumb punk? You got a forklift certification card? I didn't think so! If the OSHA inspector shows up, he will shut down this whole job if you are on that —— lift without a —— certification card. Come on; you gotta use your head for more than a hat rack. I swear you are dumber than that pile of bricks."

Frank began carrying the ninety-plus pound sacks across the lot to the storage shed. The weight wasn't bad for the first twenty sacks or so, but the combination of the number of sacks, Nevada heat, and Red had pushed Frank close to his snapping point. Red stepped in the shed as Frank placed the last of the forty sacks on the stack, and immediately it started.

"What are you doing, dipstick? How are the 'real construction workers' gonna move them now? That crap all needs to be on a pallet. That way, when somebody with a forklift card that actually works for a living comes along—boy, you aren't very smart, are you?"

The struggle within Frank raged on, Anger and Rage wanted so badly to shut this loudmouth up, but the volcano was being suppressed by the need to draw a paycheck, which helped restrain the urge to knock Red's lights out. Frank walked to pick up the empty pallet he had just created with Red close behind like a little yappy dog. The thought of Red as a Chihuahua, or even better, a wiener dog, almost brought a smile to Frank's face. Just as Frank reached down for the pallet, Red spit his tobacco juice. The world may never know whether the intention was to spit close for emphasis or actually to spit on the outstretched hand. The mischievous fourth-dimension visitor may have even altered the path of the spittle. The outcome was not good.

Frank stood up straight and looked into the wide eyes of the short, round, loudmouth man known as Red. "You seem to have dropped something! Let me put that back for you!" Frank slammed his tobacco-covered hand into the loud mouth of Red and sent him flying.

Frank looked around and noticed a crowd forming. "Should I jump on him and finish the show for the crowd or walk away?"

The trailer door opened and out stepped the job supervisor and the guy who suggested sending him to Red. "Put it down Red; the show's over. Everybody back to work." The supervisor barked, and Red dropped the two-by-four he intended on using on Frank as the crowd dispersed and went back to work.

The man with the boss swore and handed the boss some cash. "I didn't think he'd make it this long!" and walked off.

"Sorry, son. I hoped you would make it, but my brother-in-law, he is a real horse's, well, you know what he is!" The supervisor handed Frank the cash he had recently received. "Bubba bet you wouldn't make it an hour. I said you would make at least three o'clock, so here is a hundred bucks; you earned it putting up with Red for three hours. He's my wife's bum brother, so I have to put up with him, anyway; good luck to you, kid."

Frank headed back toward the Strip with an extra hundred. *If we could find a few more construction sites with jerks, we could pick up some more quick cash.* Frank had enjoyed knocking the tobacco juice out of Red and smiled as he made his way to the nearest casino. It didn't take long for Frank to figure out how to get alcohol in the casino. Most casinos had free drinks for people gambling, so he walked in, found a slot machine, and started playing. Since he looked over eighteen, no one had an issue with his gambling. He learned the hard way not to go to the bar or stop a waitress and order a drink because they wanted to see an I.D. The larger casinos would escort anyone under twenty-one attempting to drink from the premises. However, if you were involved in gambling and the waitress approached and asked for an order, it was best to act casual, like the main interest was gambling, and most of the time, they would bring you a drink. Frank also discovered it was better to keep the order limited to beer. He now looked the part of a working man in his mid-twenties and settled into the role well, not drinking excessively or blowing a lot of money at one time.

Chapter Thirty
Hello, Kandi

After a couple of shows and enough sober-up time, Frank decided to head back to the Lucky Motel. After all, there was still a 2:00 a.m. show to catch. Lust began to play in Frank's mind with the thoughts of some alone time with Kandi. *Sure, she is older, but she was all over us earlier. . . . Play the cards right and maybe . . . some free night's stay at the Lucky Motel . . . What about Bart . . . ? Forget about Bart. . . . It might be time for Kandi to replace Bart. . . . Frank the Tank, motel owner/showbiz manager . . .* What a thought.

Pulling back into the lot of the Lucky Motel, Frank made sure to park the Harley in spot number seven. After a shower, Frank slipped on one of the new job-hunting/going-out shirts he purchased earlier and got ready to head over to the motel lounge. He shoved everything else back in the duffle and locked it, still not totally comfortable with his new surroundings.

The lounge offered everything to be expected from a cheap motel lounge, from the thirty-year-old décor and dim-lights to the smell of old alcohol and cigarette smoke and a lively jazz recording playing in the background. The clientele didn't disappoint the imagination either. It had maybe a half dozen couples, three or four guys sitting at the bar, and a small group of ladies at the other end. Frank was the youngest of the twenty or so patrons by at least two decades. The women all had the look of years of heavy smoking, which didn't deter any of them, and the gentlemen all had an old-school, slicked-back look. Had Frank stepped back in time? He wouldn't have been surprised to see all these people there for Kandi's original perfor- mance, dressed exactly as they were now.

He checked the time. "Twenty minutes until showtime."

Frank had a couple of beers and then made his way to a table to the right of the stage, basically unnoticed. Each group remained in their own world until the house lights fade and the spots hit the stage, and then all eyes were on Kandi and her skimpy, twenty-year-old, show-girl costume.

Wow! She can sing! Frank thought. *At one time, she might have had a shot at the big stage.*

Frank found himself drawn into the show he was watching, almost hypnotized by the oldies but goodies performance of Kandi. *Is it my imagination, or is she singing all the old love songs this direc- tion?* Every break between songs brought a huge round of applause. In the lounge of the Lucky Motel, Kandi was a superstar, and these were her adoring fans. After several encores, Frank found himself joining in the standing ovation. Kandi made her way through the crowd of twenty or so of her most adoring fans to where he stood. She gave him a tight squeeze, pressing her scantily clad body next to his.

"I'll see you later, big boy!" she whispered as she turned to the next adoring fan and placed a kiss on his cheek.

"Best one yet, Kandi!" the older gentleman responded.

Did I hear right? See you later. . . . What? When? Frank's mind and hormones were now racing, fueled by Lust, at the thought of seeing Kandi later. He hung around the lounge until he noticed she had slipped out. Frank finished his drink and headed to room seven. *Maybe I misunderstood what she was saying.* He slipped off his boots, then laid his jeans across the dresser and climbed in the bed; no

Majik Fingers tonight, lesson learned. After the day he had, it didn't take Frank long to fall into a deep sleep.

Jingle . . . Jingle . . . Click!

"What's that? It sounds like a door being unlocked. Where am I? I must be dreaming!"

"Hey, big boy. I told you I would see you later!" came Kandi's seductive voice from the open doorway.

"I have got to be dreaming. . . . How did she get in . . . ? only a dream . . ."

The hand on his chest and the alcohol breath in his face startled him awake. That is Frank's clue that he was not dreaming, and this was actually happening.

"Relax, big boy. Kandi is going to make this a night Tank will never forget."

The smell of alcohol and cigarette smoke were nauseating, but the thoughts that Lust had racing in Frank's brain made the smell easily overlooked. The dark visitors from the fourth dimension were now swirling around lucky room seven. Between Frank and Kandi, there were at least a dozen beings, from the tiniest imp to the heavy hitters representing the kingdom of darkness. The usual power struggles were taking place with Lust and Deception leading the way down the road that leads to destruction.

Bam, Bam, Bam! "What's going on in there?"

"Oh crud, Bart!" came from Kandi's lips as the door burst open with the force of Bart's foot, revealing one distraught *manager* with a pistol in his hand and greed on his shoulder.

"That kind of action with a superstar is gonna cost extra; you gotta pay to play in Vegas, boy!"

Chapter Thirty-One
A Time to Pray

Bam!

"What was that?"

A sweet little widow in southeast Texas rolled over and clicked on her bedside lamp. The light revealed a very guilty-looking cat that had just knocked over a stack of books.

"You silly cat! Are you trying to scare the life out of me?" She laughed as the cat meowed and began grooming himself. As she turned over to go back to sleep, Holy Spirit impressed on Ms. Betty's heart: "Pray for Frank now!" A sense of urgency came over her, and she began to intercede for her grandson like she never had before. Often, the Lord would wake her to pray. She had been led to pray for Frank before—but never like this—this was life or death.

"Lord, I pray a hedge of protection above, beneath, and all around Frank! No weapon formed against him shall prosper!" Ms. Betty had no idea what was going on with her grandson in Las Vegas; she only knew it was critical that she pray.

Chapter Thirty-Two
Bye, Kandi and Bart

Reflexes sprang Frank to his feet and sent Kandi sprawling to the floor. Bart squeezed the trigger in the excitement. *Click*—no round in the chamber. Bart's intention may have been to only scare Frank and muscle extra cash out of him. He had not, however, expected the quick reflexes of an all-state line-backer. Bart's response to the rapid movement was to pull the trigger, and as soon as the hammer clicked, Frank lunged forward and hit Bart center mass with both hands. The blow sent Bart flying through the open bathroom door, across the toilet.

Bam!

"Son of a ——! You are a dead man!" Bart growled as he came to rest in the shower, wrapped in the shower curtain. Pride and Murder had now teamed up, and their goal was a bullet in this young punk. Frank hustled into his clothes, yanking on his pants, both legs at once. He snatched the bathroom door closed to slow Bart's progress. Frank slammed on his helmet and threw the strap of the duffle over his shoulder. He heard Bart struggling to free himself from the bondage of the shower curtain, swearing through the whole ordeal.

"No time for goodbye." Frank glanced and noticed Kandi still

sitting on the floor, dazed and confused. He blew her a kiss. "Boots."
Frank grabbed his boots as he heard Bart struggle with the bathroom
door. *Out the door . . . Slam it shut. . . . Dash to spot seven. . . . leg
across . . . boots in lap . . . key in . . . turn . . . kick . . . Oh crap! That hurt
the sock foot!*

The Harley roared to life! "Grab the clutch. . . . Stomp the
shifter. . . . Ouch! No time for pain!" Frank spins the Harley around.
Bam! sch . . . sch . . . "Aaaa! Oh my! Nooooo!" *Bang! Bang! Thump!
Screech!*

In the fourth dimension, one of the Heavenly Host caused a
usually sure-footed cat in Texas to knock over a stack of books a split
second before the burley manager banged on the door to room lucky
seven of a sleazy motel in Vegas. The crash of books awakened a
mighty prayer warrior, and as Ms. Betty began to pray and intercede,
angels from the Most High were loosed into action, traveling faster
than the speed of light and unseen by human eyes. The first angel
sprang into action with a blinding burst of light into the spiritual
darkness of the fourth dimension, filling the small motel room,
temporarily blinding the evil spirits and hurling them into a tizzy of
confusion. While Rage and Murder were rubbing their eyes with one
hand and swinging their battle swords frantically with the other, a
second Heavenly Warrior swooped down. Ducking, darting, and
weaving between swords and tattered leathery wings of a temporarily
blinded enemy, the angel caused Bart to get tangled in the shower
curtain, falling into the small tub, then locked the bathroom door to
impede progress further. His fellow angels sought to speed Frank's
exit.

Bam!

The front door to lucky seven was ripped open by an angry Bart,
now with Murder blazing in his eyes and vile creatures from the
fourth dimension in his head. "I'm gonna kill that worthless piece of
——." Frank spun the Harley around, motor and heart racing.

Sch . . . Sch . . . the sound of the slide was ominous as Bart cham-
bered a round in his 9 mm and took aim at the head of the young

punk that had just bested him. The first angel got Kandi to her feet and senses just in time to scream and grab Bart's arm, causing the course of the first bullet to alter slightly, ricocheting harmlessly into the night. The second shot veered high and right, lodging in the neon sign of the Lucky Motel, causing the vacancy light to flicker. The second angel helped the driver of an old Chevy slam on brakes just in time to avoid the crazy, bare-footed Harley rider, struggling with boots on his lap and a duffel bag slung over his shoulder.

Frank raced down the street as fast as the Harley would take him. After enough distance to be confident Bart was not pursuing, Frank stopped to put his boots on and collect his thoughts. As he pulled into an empty lot, he saw two police cars race by.

Wonder where they are going in such a hurry?

He slipped off his helmet to secure the duffel to the sissy bar and noticed a gouge on the right side. *Wow! That bullet was close! It must be my lucky day!*

Pride and Arrogance moved in; and rather than be scared or afraid, Frank was now even more confident that he was invincible. *I got this! I can handle whatever life throws my way.*

Looking at his watch, Frank realized that he had managed to get a couple of hours of sleep before all the excitement.

The two angels looked at each other and gave a heavenly high five. "Luck has nothing to do with it! Thank the Father for praying grandmas!"

No time for celebration; they may have won this skirmish, but the war for this young man's soul was far from over. For now, all they could do was watch from a distance until they received further orders from the Captain of the Host. While the Heavenly Host was aware that their enemy did not always work as a team, they knew all demons strive to wreak havoc and destroy humans. The ultimate goal of every evil one was to cause as many humans as possible to miss out on what they lost after the "Great Rebellion" when they were kicked out of Heaven.

Chapter Thirty-Three
Unexpected Call

Ring, Ring! The phone startled Joe and Sue awake.

"Hello . . . Hi, Mom. Mom, you do realize it is early, don't you? No, he is not here. . . . No, ma'am. We are not sure where he is right now. He took off this past Saturday, and no one around town has seen or heard from him."

Sue lay there half asleep, listening to Joe talk to his mom.

"He didn't show up in your part of the country, did he?"

Sue sat up and looked at Joe with a hopeful, questioning look. Joe shook his head, and disappointed, Sue laid back down. "No, ma'am. We haven't called the police. I know, Mom . . . Yes, Mom, he is eighteen, though. . . . What's that, Mom? You say the Lord woke you up to pray for Frank. You think he might be in trouble—a matter of life and death . . . ?"

Sue was now wide awake as she sat straight up in the bed. Her mother-in-law was one of the godliest women she knew, and if Ms. Betty was concerned, it was serious.

"Yes, ma'am. We will let you know. . . . I will. . . . Yes, ma'am. She is right here. Love you too!"

Joe handed the phone to Sue. "Hello, Ms. Betty. . . . Yes, ma'am. I have been worried; we both have. We are trying to give him some space and let him find his way back.. . ." Sue could feel the tears streaming down her cheeks, ". . . to us and . . . to . . . God." Sue nodded. "Yes, ma'am. . . . It is extremely difficult. . . . I would appreciate that very much." And Sue bowed her head as Ms. Betty began to pray for Frank that the Lord would bring him home safely.

Sue could feel the comfort of the Holy Spirit as Ms. Betty continued to pray for peace to be in their household.

"Thank you, Mom. . . . I love you too."

Sue handed Joe the phone. As he hung it up, Sue wrapped her arms around Joe and squeezed.

"I love you, Joe. . . ." she sniffed. "We just have to remember God is in control. . . . and we can't make the right choices for him. . . ."

Chapter Thirty-Four
The Boss

F rank headed toward the edge of town, opting to find a free campground and get a few more hours of sleep before continuing the job search. He did not realize how tired he was until he woke four hours after sunrise, ready for breakfast. After several more hours of unsuccessful job searching, Frank pulled into a small bar off the Strip for a cold beer. He was settling into a spot at the end of the bar when he heard a commotion. Frank noticed a very large man grabbing a scantily clad waitress who was not interested in providing the lap dance he was requesting. A couple of large bouncers emerged and attempted to persuade the intoxicated mountain of a man to leave. Frank spun around on his stool and prepared for the show he was sure was about to begin.

With a bouncer on each side, the massive mound of muscle decided he was not ready to leave. "Not without a lap dance," the man said.

The bouncers were relieved when he stood up and started to saunter toward the door. Everything was going smoothly until bouncer number one made a grave mistake and put his hand on the drunken hulk's shoulder to hurry his progress. The beast was awakened—*snap!* One broken arm and the first bouncer was out of the action! Bouncer number two attempted to subdue the mound of muscle with a choke hold. Big mistake; this only further enraged him. With a quick jerk of the neck, he slammed the back of his head into the face of bouncer number two—result: broken nose, and a second bouncer was out of the action and lying in a pool of blood. The hulk turned a cold stare toward Frank, now sitting all alone at the bar, enjoying the action, with a huge grin on his face.

"What are you looking at, punk?"

"Who, me?" Frank pointed to his own chest. "I'm just enjoying the show! I don't want any trouble with you, big guy!"

"Too late, you got trouble with me!"

The man took a step, grabbed a beer bottle, and hurled it toward Frank's head. *Crash!* The bottle smashed against the wall, narrowly missing its intended target.

"Oh God, here it comes!" Frank slid off his perch as the angry man rapidly closed the distance with fire in his eyes and fighting on his mind. Frank ducked a massive right hand and went to work driving blow after blow into the rib cage of the man, who had not prepared to face an opponent with such quick hands. After half a dozen shots to the midsection in a matter of a second, he doubled over, gasping for air, resulting from cracked ribs. Frank landed a forearm across the bridge of the man's nose, feeling the cartilage smush and blood began to gush—and down he went!

When the police arrived, several officers carried a very large drunk that had, according to several witnesses, mysteriously tripped and fallen, to jail to sleep off an overindulgence. According to police reports, a couple of bouncers had been injured while assisting the fallen patron. Frank quickly got the impression this was not the first police visit for this establishment, and they knew the man who seemed to be in charge very well.

"Boy, what is your name, and do you want a job?" A well-dressed man extended his hand toward Frank.

"What kind of job?"

"Well, to start, I need to replace a couple of bouncers that are suddenly feeling, should we say, under the weather!"

"Yes, sir! I need a job!" Frank shook his hand overenthusiastically.

"Easy there, Tiger. I need to get that hand back when you're done!" The stranger pulled his hand back. "Now, what's your name?"

"Frank, sir. But you can call me Tank! Tell me more about this job!" After all the frustrations from his previous job searches, Frank was excited to have someone offer him a job, even if he appeared to be on the shady side.

"How old are you, Tank?"

"Almost nineteen, Mr., um, I'm sorry; what do I call you, sir?"

"You, young Mr. Tank, call me Boss when you are speaking to me, and when you are speaking to someone about me, you refer to me as Big Lou or the Boss! You will understand better as time goes on!"

Frank had a sinking feeling that name was to be feared and respected in certain circles. "Okay, Mr. Big Lou. I mean Mr. Boss, sir. What exactly is my job?"

"Well, Tank, my boy, you will do what you did here this evening. You will deal with patrons that have worn out their welcome. If you do this job well and help protect my *interests*, and I see I can trust you, I may involve you in some of my other *business interests*. You see, Tank, I can use someone like you. That large gentleman threw two of my guys around, no problem, but you, ha, you, my boy, most men would have wet themselves, but, oh, my boy, you actually enjoyed it! Be honest; you liked it, didn't you?"

Frank couldn't keep the smile from his face, "Yes sir, I did kind of like it!"

The Boss stuck his hand out again, "I knew it! I could see it in your eyes! The way this works is, if you help me in, let's say, various aspects of my business, I will pay you in cash. As we build a certain, let's call it *trust*, I will give you bigger jobs. The bigger the job, the better the pay. I will treat you right; just don't ever mess with my money. If you should ever think I have treated you unfairly, talk to me, please. You'll find that I am an extremely generous man! Tank, son, just never take it upon yourself to adjust your own pay!"

Frank stood there with a bewildered look on his face, not quite sure he heard right.

"Tank, let me be clear. I am basically making you an offer you can't refuse!" The Boss chuckled at his own *Godfather* humor. "Back to what I was saying about my money . . . what I am saying is, don't ever . . . I repeat, ever—don't ever steal from me. *Do not* help yourself to my money—*Ever!* Understand?"

"Yes sir, Boss, I understand."

"Where are you staying, Tank?" The Boss knew the answer; he had already seen the Harley with the duffle outside.

"Well, sir, I don't have a place to stay right now."

"Tank, today is your lucky day! You see, this is an old bar, an old saloon from back in the early days of Vegas, with small living quarters out back, above the storeroom. I would be willing to let you work off the rent if that is agreeable with you?"

Frank agreed, mainly because he didn't wish to spend another night camping! He had the feeling he had just sold himself into the devil's service, but at least he would have a roof over his head and the promise of income.

"Pull your bike around back, and you will see the rear entrance at the top of the stairs. Here is a key. The front door is in the back of the storeroom. There are usually other activities, such as private parties or special card games and such happening in the storeroom, so when you are not working, it is better to use the rear entrance and avoid the storeroom, you know, for privacy and discretion." The boss continued talking, but Frank's mind dwelled on the thought of a *special* store-room out back. "Tank, pay attention! When I'm telling you something, it is important to listen!"

"Yes, sir! Sorry, Boss. I got a little distracted."

"Anyway, Tank, I was saying, you listening? 'Cause I am not gonna repeat myself again."

"Yes, Boss. I am listening. I won't let it happen again!"

"Tank, when you are working, or anytime you are in the presence of our customers up front, you will wear one of our black polo shirts. I'll get you a few in a second. Anytime you use the storeroom entrance to the apartment, you must be wearing one of those shirts. Our back-room *guests* value their privacy, and it provides a certain, let's call it, *comfort level*. Basically, the shirt lets them know you work for me, and it's okay for you to be back there. Now, follow me to the office." The two step into a well-decorated office and the boss hands Frank several nice polos. "When we are done here you can move your bike, get settled, and come down for work in an hour or so, or whenever you are ready." The boss took a seat behind a highly polished antique wooden desk. "For now," the boss continued, puffing a freshly lit cigar." You will be helping with security upfront, basic bouncer stuff, maintaining order, removing any troublemakers peacefully, whenever possible, and reasonable force whenever necessary. Make sure nobody gets out of hand with one of our girls." As if for clarity the boss fixed his eyes on Frank and blew smoke from the corner of his mouth." The girls will let you know if someone is out of hand. You will always be working with at least one other bouncer. Never try to handle a situation alone; always work with your team. Most of the time, people have enough *respect* not to cause trouble, but occasionally, we get a knot-head like today, and well, that's why we are having this conversation. I like what I saw and think we can be of mutual benefit to one another."

The boss nodded toward the door. "Get settled and come back down in an hour or so, ready to work with the shirt on, okay?"

Frank noticed the shirts were a nice black polo with the bar's logo and the word "Security" embroidered in gold on the right side.

Chapter Thirty-Five

New Place, New Job, Life Is Good Again

Frank pulled the Harley around to the rear entrance and made his way upstairs to his new home. While it was by no means a five-star hotel, the apartment was not exactly a dump either. He had all the basics: a double bed, dresser, nightstand, and small color television. It also had a small kitchenette with a fridge, cooktop, and a small microwave. Frank noticed a small bathroom with a sink, toilet, and shower. The apartment had all the basics to be called self-contained; Frank had to admit he is pleasantly surprised. It even had decent artwork hanging on the walls. The fourth-dimension beings kept Frank's mind swirling with excitement at the potential of this new home. It was as close to paradise as an eighteen-year-old male could imagine—living in a cool bachelor place, above a bar, with a *special* storeroom and a paying job—life was good, really good! For the first time since he left Iowa, Frank felt comfortable enough with his surroundings to unpack the duffle bag and put his clothes away in the dresser.

"I can actually spend more than one night here!" He then realized he had not slept in the same spot two nights in a row since he left home.

After a quick shower, Frank got ready to report for his new job, remembering the polo. The fit was tight enough to show off Frank's size but not so tight to cut off his circulation. He stepped out of the apartment onto a glass-enclosed landing, realizing he can see and not be seen. He made his way downstairs, behind the two-way mirror hall, quickly noticing the backroom clientele were not run-of-the-mill bar customers. The people in this room had lots of money. Frank could see a stage with several scantily dressed women dancing very provocatively before a dozen tables with well-dressed men and women. Lust and Perversion were running rampant in the play-ground of Frank's imagination. Off to one side, he noticed a couple of tables with high-dollar poker games going on. The other side contained *very private booths*. Frank found out their purpose from one of the other bouncers standing discreetly at the bottom of the stairs just inside the storeroom.

"The clients watch the dancers. . . . When they see something they like, well, that's what the *booths* are for. . . . Anything goes for the right price. . . . single guys . . . couples . . . you name it! Oh! By the way, I'm Lee, but everybody calls me Bull."

"Frank, but everybody calls me Tank."

Bull continued, "Back here, it is pretty laid back; not a lot of trou-ble. Main thing: make sure no uninvited guests wander in from the front. You know these folk like their privacy, and they pay well to maintain it! The backroom clients have their own entrance and exit toward the rear of the building."

Frank had noticed several high-end cars outback where he parked the Harley but failed to see the rear entrance.

"Anyway, Boss says you will be working the front tonight. . . . more of your average bar crowd, kind of a mix of locals and tourists looking for something off the main strip. Every once in a while, some-body will have too much to drink and try to get too friendly with one of the girls. Bull stopped and gave Frank a look, oddly similar to the one the boss had given earlier. "The girls will let you if someone is out of line. Oh yeah! Bull continued as if remembering a key detail, watch the dance floor, especially tonight. It will be crowded. It never fails; somebody will accidentally bump someone and spill a drink, then they want to fight." Bull walked in the direction of a hallway that led to the bar up front. "You will be working with Ray. Everybody calls him Cool-Ray. He is a good one to learn from; he can usually talk a situation down, but Ray can also handle business and bust heads when he needs to. He will have your back if you need him."

Frank thanked Bull for the info and made his way through a winding hall. Upfront, he found Ray sitting toward the back, drinking a cup of water. The crowd was on the younger side, and the room was full of high-energy dance music.

"This is awesome!" Frank was ready to grab a beer and join the party.

"No drinking on the job!" It was difficult for Frank to hear Cool-Ray, but he understood the no-drinking part. The spirits swarming around Frank were totally at home in this atmosphere. He had to remind himself that this was a job and not a party.

The night was uneventful. The only thing close to exciting was when a couple of drunk college guys got into a shoving match. Cool-Ray quickly stepped up with Tank at his back and calmed the situation down by having the two tough guys shake hands and go their separate ways. Frank spent the next few nights working with and learning from Ray. He was convinced life couldn't get much better than this. He worked in a bar, lived above a high-class, anything-goes party, and had access to all the women and alcohol he could want in his off time. In no time, Frank managed to be *promoted* to the back room. He was even making extra cash in the *private booths*, dancing for bachelorette parties, and entertaining wealthy young socialites.

The Boss also had new jobs for Frank that better utilized his particular skill sets. The Boss would send Frank to collect debt, make deliveries and pickups, anything where muscle was required. The more Frank worked for the Boss, the more he learned about the business. The principle of business was simple: If you owe the Boss money, there are three options: First, pay when you agree to pay; second, in certain situations, a person can work off their debt. Or the final option is, Frank or whomever the muscle may be, will make things very ugly for you.

The third was Frank's favorite when he ran across a tough guy that wanted to take their chances. The Boss permitted him, in certain situations, to use the force necessary to get the point across.

"Frank, I want you to drive me to a special poker game tonight. We will be taking the Rolls and leaving from the backlot at 11:30, and Frank, dress nice and don't be late." The boss appeared to be in a good mood, but Frank could tell by the tone of his voice that he was serious about the don't be late part.

Frank put on his best clothes and headed downstairs ten minutes early to get the car ready. It did not take him long to learn the Boss was not the type of man you kept waiting. Behind the wheel, Frank followed the Boss' directions from the backseat.

"Turn into this gate," the Boss said. Frank recognized the lot from his first night in Vegas. ". . . pull over to the left side once you get on the lot." Frank looked inside the guard shack.

"Yep, there's Bobby!" he thought out loud. Bobby looked, recognized Frank, and looked away quickly, without making eye contact. Frank parked the Rolls, and the Boss waited for him to come around and open the door.

"Go, wait in the security area, this may take a few hours. . . . You will know when it's time to go! Tank, remember, don't make me wait, understand?"

"Yes, sir, I understand!"

Frank entered the security door and found a large room full of muscle and security monitors. He quickly realized the VIP room was full of the wealthiest, most powerful men and women in the Vegas area. Frank noticed the parking lots, as well as all the exits, were monitored by cameras.

"This is why Bobby was so confident that first night."

The grin of a schoolboy briefly crossed his face as he remembered that first night. It had gone as quickly as it came when Frank the Tank realized all eyes were on the newcomer, him. Giving his best tough-guy nod, he strolled to a corner with a view of the security monitors.

An extensive buffet table was set up for all the security personnel as they sat around exchanging stories from the lifestyle around the rich and famous. Frank listened as these seasoned veterans bragged of exploits while doing their "jobs" and soon learned he had earned a measure of respect with this crowd simply because he worked for the Boss. Talk of busting heads to collect "debts" and reaping other benefits from their employment had Frank giddy with excitement over the future possibilities his new job might offer. According to several, the Boss was a great guy as long as you stayed on his good side. "You don't ever want to be on his bad side" was the popular consensus.

As the night wore on into the early morning, the crowd was gradually thinning until only the Boss and two others remained. A few more hands and the Boss was placing a large amount of cash in the case he entered with, and Frank was sure that it was time to leave. The Boss met Frank at the Rolls and joined him in the front seat, placing the case on the seat between them.

"Tank, my boy, lady luck was very good to me tonight. . . . The cards fell in my favor for sure."

Back at the bar, Frank started upstairs.

"Tank, here's your pay for tonight." The Boss handed Frank five crisp one-hundred-dollar bills.

"Thank you, Boss, sir! I uh . . ."

"Tank, go to bed. Get your rest. I have a big job for you tonight!"

Chapter Thirty-Six
Love My Job

F rank rushed downstairs, full of excitement over the thought of the big job.

"The Boss wants to see you in his office."

Tank recognized Cool-Ray's voice and turned around, "Thanks, bro."

"Tank, watch your back tonight!"

In the office, he received instructions. "Tank, I need you to collect from a . . ." the Boss used a stream of expletives. "This . . ." (more expletives) "—— wants to party with a few of our female employees. You see, it is bad that he got rough with the girls but even worse, he owes me a lot of money! If he even looks at you funny, you . . ." The Boss instructed him to rearrange this guy's parts in a way Frank was sure was next to impossible.

Arriving at the location the Boss had given, it didn't take long for Frank to locate the gentleman. He matched the Boss's description perfectly: forties, balding, dressed like a seventies disco reject, surrounded by several *hired ladies*.

He approached the table. "The Boss sent me," Frank spoke, using his best tough-guy voice.

The gentleman Frank dubbed Disco Dan was shaken but quickly recovered and strove to maintain cool in the presence of his *dates*. "Uh, yes. I have that, uh, stuff he wanted to borrow in my room. If you would like to wait with my friends while I fetch it . . ."

"That's okay. . . ." Frank nodded and smiled his dimpled smile at the girls. "I will walk with you."

"Aw!" the girls sighed in harmony.

"It is all right, ladies; have another round on my tab!"

Upstairs in the room, Frank watched Disco Dan carefully as he retrieved several large stacks of hundred-dollar bills from the wall safe. "You can count it if you need to?"

"It's all good; I'm sure you don't want me to have to come back!"

As Frank stuck the cash in the bank bag the Boss had given him, he saw a flash in his peripheral vision. *This fool pulled a knife he had hidden in the safe!* Frank would laugh as he later told the Boss. Rage took over, and the gentleman was out cold after the first punch to the face, but Frank held him up with one hand and unleashed his wrath with the other. He allowed Disco Dan to slump to the floor as he picked up his former would-be attacker's knife and slipped it in his back pocket. Turning to walk out, he remembered the girls downstairs in the lounge. "A little something for their . . . service . . ." Frank chuckles as he removed Disco's wallet and lightened it by several hundred dollars.

"Ladies, I am sorry, your *date* wasn't feeling well and decided to turn in early."

"Oh no!" they responded in mock disappointment; everything was all better when Frank placed the cash on the table.

"He said to enjoy the rest of your evening on him."

"Won't you stay and party with us, please?"

"Sorry, ladies. I'm working tonight. Maybe another time!" Frank turned and walked out as tempting as it was, remembering he did not want to keep the Boss waiting.

Chapter Thirty-Seven
Mr. Robinson

"You, son, are a sinner, in need of a Savior!"

The hair on the back of his neck stood up as Frank noticed the source of the voice standing between him and the Harley. "Are you talking to me?"

Frank could feel his blood starting to boil as he closed the distance. "Who in the hell are you, and why are you judging me?" Frank yelled from a few feet away.

The voice remained oddly calm. "Everyone calls me Robinson, friend, and I am not judging you. The Word says, 'For all have sinned and fall short of the glory of God' (Romans 3:23 NIV)."

Frank clenched his teeth, and something within him hissed, "I don't care. . . . I know about Jesus!"

"Even the evil ones that torment you know about Jesus, but you need to know Him as Savior!"

Frank glanced around. "Right now, you are the one that needs to know a savior!"

Frank was only inches away as he towered over Robinson, who was looking up into his face, unblinking.

"The Lord loves you, and He died to set you free from the bondage you are currently in!" The demons swirling around were fuming and in a frenzy. "All you have to do is—" *Ouf!* A sucker punch to the midsection caught Robinson off guard as he stepped back and knelt to catch his breath.

Frank grabbed the knife from his pocket, and as he stepped toward Robinson, he heard the words, "No weapon that is formed against thee shall prosper" (Isaiah 54:17, KJV).

Frank lunged, intending on slicing and dicing this street preacher, as an unseen warrior grabbed his arm and stopped him in his tracks. The warrior's booming voice served notice to all the ears in the fourth dimension, "This one is off limits!"

The evil ones with Frank were outnumbered five to one by seasoned warriors of the Heavenly Host who were at the ready, swords drawn, and prepared for battle. Despite the desires of his traveling companions to shed some human blood, Frank slipped the knife back into his pocket. He spat in the direction of the man of God and headed toward the Harley. He had the overwhelming urge to make a speedy getaway, feeling intimidated by a small framed street preacher. Later, in the retelling of the story to the Boss, Frank thought it best not to mention his encounter with Robinson. His brain had not yet processed the events of their meeting, and he knew he could not even begin to explain, so for now, only two people knew.

Life was good. The Boss was very generous when compensating for a job well done. Anything Frank wanted was available, and right now, his wants were driven by Lust, Greed, Seduction, Addiction, and a host of other evil ones. Nice clothes, a party life, and plenty of women were a thin veil for a life spiraling out of control. "Whenever the Boss needs a job done, Tank is his guy! Tank doesn't mind getting his hands dirty!" Frank was building quite a reputation in the dark side of Sin City. Whatever the job, he would do it. No questions asked—debt collection, package delivery, party security. All the *muscle* at the bar enjoyed making collections with Frank.

"It's like Tank wants them not to pay; then he punishes them and makes them pay anyway!" The other guys enjoyed reporting to the Boss about Frank's work. "Boss, we just watch the door and let Tank work; it is a thing of beauty, Boss."

Chapter Thirty-Eight
Special Job

"Tank, my boy, I have a special job for you!" Frank had grown accustomed to those words as the Boss grinned his direction. He seemed to take great joy in giving Frank these assignments. "I need you to collect a debt from a young lady! You know the deal, Tank. She either pays her debt in full, or she can choose to *work off* her debt at several of my *special parties!* You can take the Porsche; just bring me the money or her answer by noon tomorrow. If she chooses to work, I need her tomorrow night."

Address and keys in hand, Frank headed for the parking lot. It was great when the Boss let him take the Porsche. This type of collection wasn't as risky and didn't pay as well, so the car was a nice benefit. He was learning his way around Vegas and this street name was familiar for some strange reason. *Oh, well, a job is a job!* he thought, as he slipped behind the wheel of the Porsche. *Make this collection, then cruise the Strip in the Porsche.*

When Frank saw the Buick with its flat tire, he knew why the address seemed familiar. "Dang! That's the last thing I need to deal with; maybe she isn't home!" Frank muttered as he knocked on the door.

"Tex, I mean, um, Tank, how are you? Looks like Vegas is treating you well!" Veronica snarked as she looked past Frank to the new Porsche in the driveway.

"Hi, Veronica. Sorry, this isn't a social visit."

"Yeah, I heard you were working for . . . him. . . . I wondered if he would send you; guess now I know!"

"Can I come in?"

"Why? You don't want any witnesses? I've heard how you deal with people that don't pay your boss!" Frank could see the fire in the redhead's eyes as she leaned forward and pointed to her nose. "Go ahead! Hit me, break it, 'cause I don't have the money, and I sure ain't working at one of his parties! Yeah, I know how you and your boss work, so go ahead. Hit me and get it over with!"

"Shut up! I ain't gonna hit you!" He snapped as he pushed his way past a fiery redhead with her fist clenched, eyes wincing, as she braced herself, almost expecting him to punch her. "I need to think for a minute!"

The thought of Veronica being treated the way some of the girls working off debts at the boss's parties were made Frank sick to his stomach. "Do you have any of the money . . . ? How much do you owe? Maybe I can help?"

"Tank . . . I am *not* paying anymore. . . . I have already paid almost double what I borrowed; I just haven't always been on time. You know, dealing with your boss isn't like the bank, not much grace period! Tank, wake up! It isn't about the money; he wants to force me to work for him. You know my deal; I decide who I have sex with, remember!"

Frank sat on the couch that had been his bed that first night in Vegas. "The boss always gets what he wants! You know I can't hurt you!" He raked his fingers through his hair, and she could see the anguish on his face. "I can't. . . . But the next guy can . . . and will . . . hurt you without a second thought!"

Was that a tear she saw on his cheek? He stood and paced around the small apartment.

"Tank, I'm a big girl. I can handle it!"

He spun around and took Veronica by the shoulders, "No! You can't handle it! You don't know what the people working for him are capable of!"

Frank thought of some of the things he had done to make the boss happy, but it was different when it was someone you know. "No! Listen, this is the plan. Pack your stuff! I will try to get your car running; the boss isn't expecting to hear from me until tomorrow. You get in that Buick and drive; you drive until you can't go anymore, all the way back to Kansas. Whenever I come back, or whoever he sends, you be gone, anywhere but here!"

Rather than an evening cruising the Strip in the new Porsche, it was an evening under the hood of an old Buick. "I swear, somebody pulled the coil wire off and let the air out of the tire."

Frank was starting to get the revelation that what the boss really wanted was Veronica turning tricks or maybe even making porn flicks for him. Based on what he had seen and done for the boss, this was no surprise. After the Buick was purring like a kitten almost, Frank gave Veronica a couple hundred and then remembered Tiny's card.

"Check this guy and his wife out in Denver; they are good people!"

For some strange reason, Frank knew they would not mind.

Chapter Thirty-Nine
Unhappy Boss

Frank headed toward the boss's office before lunch. "I'll tell him she wasn't home. . . . Then, when whoever goes back, well, she will be long gone."

He walked in and sat down like he always did to bring the boss up to speed on the situation. "Yes, sir! I went to the address. I waited around, even went back a couple of times, no sign of her anywhere."

"Tank, did you talk to the neighbors?"

"Nobody had anything to say, Boss."

"Are you sure she wasn't home?"

"Oh, yes, sir, positive!"

Bam! The boss slammed his fist on the desk; Frank jumped back, almost falling out of his chair.

"Oh, wait, Boss. . . " he stuttered as he found himself staring down the barrel of a .45.

"Wait? For what? For you to tell me more of these lies? I know what goes on. I know every step you make, Tank. I have eyes everywhere! You take me for a fool? What happened? You go in, get a little freebie, then help her leave town? You *fixed* her car. What, do you think the wire just fell off? I had her, Tank! Do you have any idea how much a redhead brings in the adult film industry?"

"Boss, sir, I'm sorry. I'll, um, I will make it up to you, Boss! Whatever it costs! I promise, sir!"

"It's not about the money! You lied to me, Tank! Now get out of here before I kill you myself!"

Frank slid back toward the door, eyes fixed on the pistol, apologizing profusely.

"Out! I'll figure out how you can make it right later!" The boss was angrier than Frank had ever seen. "I want you out of my sight while I figure out what this is going to *cost* you! Trust, Tank. You betrayed my trust!"

The boss lowered his aim from Frank's head and motioned toward the exit. "Out now!"

He didn't need to be told twice.

Kicking the Harley, Frank's mind was swirling. *What will it take to get back on the boss's good side?* Maybe a ride in the desert would help clear his head. The fourth dimension around Frank buzzed with activity as he struggled with the events of the past few weeks. As the sun began to set, images of the things he had done for the boss flooded his mind. *What would the boss require to get back on his good side? Could it be any worse?* Frank had crossed lines with a man he did not want to cross. The darkness he was now experiencing in the desert, away from the city lights, was a direct reflection of his life right now. The glimmer of light from a house in the distance was more than life offered right now. Depression, Discouragement, and Hopelessness all began to work in Frank's mind, magnifying everything. Out of the darkness, a grotesque, almost human, figure darted in front of his helmet. Its coloring was somehow actually the same as the black lacquer paint of the Harley's tank.

The smell of sulfur was overwhelming. Frank jerked the handlebars to the right to shake the image that now appeared to be in the helmet with him. A sight seldom seen by human eyes, Frank was face to face with the evil bent on destroying him as the fourth-dimension evil stared him in the face. The Harley started into a 60-mile-an-hour skid. Jerking the bars back to the left and trying to shake the vile creature served only to separate bike and rider. Now airborne, no life flashing before the eyes or other near-death experience, the only thought was, *This is going to hurt a lot!* Bike sliding, rider flying in slow motion, demons circling like vultures moving in on roadkill—then—darkness.

"What in the world? Did you see that?" A couple, just about to get in the car and head into town, witnessed the crash as it unfolded, minus the fourth-dimension excitement. "You go inside and call an ambulance, and I will go check on the rider!"

Frank could hear the wail of a siren then muffled voices; he could feel the burn of road rash on his shoulders and the vice tightening around his head. Frank wanted to scream, but his voice would not work, and his eyes would not open. *Ouch!* He felt the stick of a paramedic's needle, then a warm sensation went up his left arm, then he was out again.

Chapter Forty
What's Going On?

"Hey, wake up! Come on! Here's the guy that has been causing trouble for the boss, and tonight is our night to make him pay!" Frank was relieved he knew that voice; it must have all been a bad dream, the crash, the boss with the gun, and the whole Veronica thing!

"The boss said one of this guy's people is going to hand him over to give us a 'signal' or something."

Frank's mind still felt fuzzy, and his surroundings seemed blurry. He didn't know this place. . . . some type of woods . . . or oasis . . . or maybe a garden. The thoughts were racing and adrenaline was pumping as he struggled to sort through the events of the last two days: *How much is real . . . ? Has it all been a dream . . . ? Did somebody slip him some bad dope? Well, this all seems real. . . . going to get some troublemaker in the middle of the night . . . nothing strange about that.* He went with a mob of people, most of whom he didn't know, getting some guy who always surrounds himself with at least a dozen or so men . . . no problem . . . just go with the flow. . . . Maybe if the boss were upset earlier, this would make it right.

"We are getting close; remember to watch for the sign!"

There was that familiar voice again, Frank still wasn't quite sure of what was happening. "Oh, well. No time for this! Got to focus . . . There it is! That guy just walked in the middle of the group and kissed that dude with the beard on the cheek—that has to be the sign!" Frank's mind raced as his body sprang into action. "This is it. If this guy is so bad . . . and I get him first . . . The boss will be happy. . . . Bam! Back in his good graces!" Frank broke away from the mob and made a grab for the troublemaker.

Flash!

Out of the corner of his eye, he saw—

"Owwww! My ear! You cut off my freakin' ear!" *That was a sword! He had a sword! Who carries a stinkin' sword?* Frank went to his knees, his mind swirling, as he grabs the side of his head where his ear used to be and looked in shock at his bloody ear laying on the ground. He felt a hand on his shoulder as someone bent down and picked up his ear—it was him! The guy they were after. . . . *What is the deal? This dude is sick! He is taking my ear as a dang trophy!* Looking up, Frank found himself looking into eyes filled, not with hate, anger, or even vengeance, but sympathy. *What is he doing? He just . . . he just put my stinkin' ear back on. . . . This is a dream. . . . those eyes . . . I know . . . that face. . . .*

"Doctor, he just opened his eyes!"

Frank knew the face staring down at him from somewhere and the voice; he just could not place where.

What's going on? Why can't I move? Why are all these people around me? Hey, this is a hospital! What the heck? Thoughts swirl through Frank's pounding head.

"It is all right, Mr. Robinson. Right now, opening his eyes is only a reflex."

Reflex? Frank thought. *I'll show you reflex! Let me get my arm loose, and I'll start kicking butt until I get answers!*

"You see, he has suffered a serious blow to the head, and his body needs to rest. So we will keep him sedated and let him get that rest.

Even though his eyes are open, his mind is still out of it. He is in dreamland and not aware of any of this. It is lucky for him that you were so close; he would not have had much of a chance in the middle of nowhere."

Robinson remembered their first meeting as he leaned down: "Luck didn't have anything to do with it. It was the Good Lord that brought our paths together again!" The street evangelist whispered just loud enough for Frank to hear. "He's not done with you yet, my young friend."

Robinson put his hand lightly on Frank's shoulder and softly prayed.

That's it! Frank remembered the last time he had looked into that face; he punched this guy right in the gut with everything he had. *What's his deal?* As Frank laid on his back, his body motionless and his mind moving at a million miles per hour, he struggled to separate what was happening from the dream world. He could breathe independently, and his ears were vividly aware of hospital sounds all around, but nothing would move.

"Hey, scum! Get up! You are going before the Governor!"

Frank shook his head as he was awakened by a couple of guys in some type of weird uniform. He noticed he was wearing some light kind of robe, but it was different from any hospital gown.

"What's going on?"

"Get moving, punk! You have a date with the judicial system!"

Frank's mind was racing. *That's it! These guys are cops!*

"The Governor is going to continue his tradition of pardoning one of you scum!" the first uniform snapped with scorn in his voice. "You don't stand a chance; everyone knows how cruel and wicked you are. . . . And now . . . Your time to pay has come!"

The two dragged Frank in chains to a podium overlooking a large courtyard that was rapidly filling with people.

Since when do they have court outside? Frank's brain was still fuzzy.

The guards kept a tight grip just in case he had any thoughts of trying to escape. Frank glanced across at the other candidate for release.

"I'm screwed!" Frank said. There was something vaguely familiar, but he couldn't place him. Another guy, obviously the Governor, joined them and began by quieting the crowd.

"It is the custom of you Jews for me to release to you one prisoner, so today you will decide! Who would you have me release? One of the most notorious criminals in this region, convicted of murder; this scum, the one known as Barabbas?" As he pointed to Frank, Frank lunged toward the crowd against the chains and tried to spit on them as the guards gave a quick yank. "Or, perhaps, your King—the King of the Jews—Jesus. Guilty of healing the sick!"

The crowd, now on the verge of a riot, shouted, "Give us Barabbas! We want Barabbas!" (John 18:40 NIV).

The Governor nodded, and the two guards began unlocking the chains.

"Hurry up, already!" Frank barked eager to leave before the Governor changed his mind.

Frank, aka Barabbas, ran toward his thug buddies, who were already plotting their next crime. As he celebrated his newfound freedom, he could hear as the Governor pleaded with the crowd, "But what about Jesus?"

The crowd, in a frenzy, shouted, "Crucify Him! Crucify Him!" (John 19:15 NIV).

Beep. Beep. Beep. The sound of the monitor in the dimly lit hospital room was almost deafening. Frank was able to open his eyes just enough to realize he was all alone and still unable to move. No crowds, no Governor, no guards, just Frank alone with his thoughts. *It should have been me! I'm the guilty one—I deserve to be punished for what I've done—he took my place!* Then, the room went black—he was out again.

Thump. Splat. Aaaahhhh. Thump. Thump! Frank woke up with a hammer in his hand and something warm and wet splattering in his face. "What's the deal? What's happening now? What am I building?" Frank, looking down, his mind racing for answers, continued, "That's a hand—a human hand! It's still alive—He's still alive!"

"Let's go, soldier! Finish the feet!"

Immediately, the story was familiar, but this was not Mr. Stone's Sunday school class. These were not words on a page. Frank could feel the hammer's wooden handle in his hand. The warm wetness on his face—the splattering blood of—of Jesus!

"Why can't I wake up? Am I asleep . . . ? This is way too real to be a dream!"

"Soldier, if you can't finish the feet, then move. . . . We got two more after him!"

Frank wanted to run, to wake up, to get away, to be anywhere but here. His mind wanted one thing, but his body moved and did the job of a Roman soldier.

Moving to the feet, the commander that had been urging him to finish shoved another spike into Frank's hand. *Whop! Whop! Whop!* His arms were going through the motions, his stomach turning. This was too real, too vivid to be a dream. Frank could feel the sweat on his face mixing with the blood splatter. The temperature was not oppressively hot; he would guess mid-seventies, with no wind. The air felt heavy, almost pressing down on Frank's entire body. The sound of the enormous crowd and their taunts drowned out most of the other sounds except for the pleadings of the other two being put to death, begging to be spared. Frank could smell the body odor of the other soldiers as they stood up the Cross. *Thud!* He heard the cry of agony as it fell in place and the shoulders of the victims were dislocated. He also smelled blood and death—this was a place of death. His senses were on overload.

"He saved others; let's see Him save Himself—this is the King of the Jews—ha! Some king!" The crowds taunted and jeered. Even one of the other criminals being crucified joined in.

Frank stepped into a dice game for the robe as they waited for the three men hanging on the crosses to die. He grabbed a stick and shoved a sponge on it when the one called Jesus said He was thirsty. Frank soaked it in sour wine and stuck it in His face. His mind was unable to object as his body performed all these motions.

"If I didn't know it was a man . . ."

The face and head were twice the size of a man's. His back and sides were shredded, torn apart by a lead-tipped whip in the hands of a master punisher. He wanted so badly to look away, yet Frank's eyes were drawn to those eyes, sunken deep in that swollen head. They were not eyes full of hate or anger but eyes filled with compassion. The eyes of a man on a mission!

"He . . . He just said, 'Father forgive them. . . .'"

Beep! Beep! Beep! Frank recognized the sound of the hospital and voices, familiar voices. "The doctor says his body is fine, except for the road rash. . . ."

That sounds like dad. . . . When did he get here?

"He says there is plenty of brain activity. . . ."

Of course, there is brain activity, Mom! I just can't wake up for some reason.

". . . so they don't think he has any permanent damage. We just have to pray and wait for him to wake up!"

Hey, who are you two talking to? Nothing, no response. *I said, who are you talking to?* Still, nothing. *Fine, don't answer. I'll open my eyes and see for my dang self! Okay, eyes open. Open now. . . . Come on! Since when is opening your eyes so difficult!*

After a great deal of mental coaxing, Frank's eyes popped open. *Wait! There is a set of eyes staring back!*

"Mr. Joe, Mrs. Sue, he is awake—Frank, can you hear me? If you can hear me, blink."

Nothing, not even a flutter. Just a blank stare at the ceiling. He may not have been able to blink, but he found himself looking into eyes filled with compassion. The same compassion he had recently seen hanging on a Cross. The last time he had looked into those eyes, they were filled with hurt. *Oh, Stacy . . . I am so sorry. . . . I messed up so bad. . . . I was a jerk!* Frank wanted so badly to grab Stacy and hold her tight; only his arms refused to cooperate.

"It is okay, dear, the doctor said when he is ready, his brain just isn't ready to wake up. Right now, it is letting his body rest."

But I do want to wake up, Mom! Then the room went black. . . . He was out, yet again.

Chapter Forty-One
Darkness

"Darkness . . . darkness everywhere . . . It is barely even noon!" Frank, now the captain of the guard, struggled with what he was seeing. In his current state, he had all his memories of being Frank, but he also had all the memories of a Roman soldier in Jerusalem, almost two thousand years ago. As chief over executions, he had vivid memories of watching many men be crucified. When men were knocking on death's door, they would proclaim their innocence, curse their accusers, curse soldiers, curse God. This guy was different. He had refused the drugged wine, the one thing that may have eased the pain. Rather than curse God, He had asked for forgiveness, not for anything He may have done but forgiveness for those mocking Him! Now the darkness; it had been dark for almost three hours, in the middle of the afternoon. It was no ordinary darkness, like night-time darkness. This darkness had a heavy, oppressive feel about it. Frank struggled with all of the memories bouncing around in his head. Every time he had ever messed up in his life, every failure, every sin he had ever committed was now fresh in his mind. The darkness was not only an absence of light; but it was also missing any sign of hope or feeling of good. The darkness was weighted with evil and despair.

"It is finished!" Jesus said. Then He bowed His head and died.

Fear swept over Frank and the guards when the earth began to quake.

Somewhere between the past and the present, the natural dimension and the supernatural fourth dimension, conscience and unconsciousness, Frank's mind raced. He had been wounded, had his ear cut off by a sword, then healed by the one they were arresting. He had been on trial and set free, and the innocent one was accused and sentenced in his place. He had nailed Jesus to the Cross.

Mind racing, he thought, *I hurt Him. . . . He healed me. . . . I deserved to die for my sins. He took my place. . . . It was me, my sins that nailed Jesus to the Cross. . . . Men mocked Him. . . . I mocked Him. . . . He asked the Father to forgive them—He forgave me!*

"Surely, this is the Son of God. . . ." the head soldier cried out in a loud voice, as a young man in a hospital bed desperately struggled to open his eyes.

The Host of Heavenly Warriors knew they were gaining ground in the spiritual war for the soul of this human. His spiritual eyes were opening to the true love of the Father.

The other four people in the room were gathered around Frank's bed anxiously praying when his eyelids began to slowly flutter.

I get it now! I never understood in my heart the price He paid for me! Now realizing that his mind and body were awakening and coming back from an incredible, eye-opening, life-changing journey, Frank's brain began to process the voices in the room. *Mom? Dad? Wait, how did you know? When . . . How long have you guys been here? How long have I been here?* Frank had so many questions, but the dryness of his mouth and throat made speech difficult. "Water please!" he croaked out in a craggy whisper.

Joe, Sue, and Stacy were so overwhelmed with emotion. Sue quickly grabbed the straw and water glass from the rolling tray beside the bed. Joe raised the bed slightly to help his son take a sip of water and better see everyone in the room. Joe could tell by the confused expression on Frank's face as he glanced at each person there in the room that he was full of questions.

Keeping his voice low and slow, Joe began to shed some light on recent events, "Three nights ago, you had an accident on your motorcycle! Mr. Robinson here, oh, you don't know Mr. Robinson," Joe continued as the street evangelist stepped forward and grasped Frank's hand. "Mr. Robinson stepped out of his front door just in time to see you fly over the handlebars!"

"We've met!" Frank interrupted in a gravely tone just above a whisper. "Sorry about . . ." Frank continued looking into the eyes of the man that saved his life as Robinson held up a hand, giving the stop sign.

"That is forgotten history," Robinson insisted.

Joe glanced back and forth then continued, "Anyway, he was there immediately, and his lovely wife called the paramedics, who said you could have bled to death if . . ."

Joe cleared his throat, and Sue spoke, "Son, you could have been laying out in the middle of nowhere for hours. . . ." Her voice trailed off.

Joe continued, "Mr. Robinson, who has been here almost the entire time, tracked us down using your driver's license. Turns out, he knows Officer Krantz back home. Anyway, he called."

Sue interrupted again, "Stacy had stopped by to see if we had heard from you when we received the call from Mr. Robinson. She was determined to come with us!"

Frank looked toward Stacy. Stacy shrugged sheepishly, smiled anxiously, and gave a shoulder-high quick wave. She was now questioning her decision to come, remembering their last night together. Stacy knew how her heart felt, but what were Frank's feelings? *Would things be different? Had a close call with death been enough to get his attention?*

A dimpled smile and the look in his eyes reminded her of the young boy her heart was drawn to so many years ago. She was right to be there even if it was nothing more than as a friend. Stacy slid over to the side of the bed and took Frank's hand, being mindful of the IV. She leaned over and kissed his swollen cheek, tears welling up in her eyes again. Frank looked deep into her eyes and spoke straight from his heart to her heart, "I am so sorry! I love you, Stacy! Can you forgive me?"

She nodded, tears streaming down her cheeks. She slowly withdrew her hand. She loved him more than she could express with words, but he had crushed her heart more than he could imagine. That last night together had destroyed her trust and made her feel insecure and unsafe. Time would tell if he had truly changed.

"I'm going to need everyone to step out to the hall for a bit while we check Frank," the doctor said, as he and nurse came into the room. After an intense fifteen minutes, the family was allowed back in to hear the verdict and ask their questions. "If everything continues to positively progress, I am going to release you in a day or two, but we want make sure you're ready. I would like you to get out of bed and start trying to walk up and down the halls for short walks until you regain your strength and balance. Everything looks good, no bones appear to be broken, no internal bleeding or infections; however, your body has been beaten up pretty badly and will need time to heal. It is normal for you to be sore, but I do not feel there will be any long-term effects. Also, you will need to follow up with your family physician when you get home, just to be on the safe side."

The doctor jotted a few notes in Frank's chart and excused himself to finish his rounds. Mr. Robinson walked to the bedside to say his goodbyes. Frank shook his hand and started, "I'm sorry. You saved my——"

Mr. Robinson put his index finger to his own lips and stopped him. In a tone only the two of them could hear Robinson spoke, "My young brother, I didn't save your life. The Father merely allowed me to play a small part in the great plan He has for your life. If you will seek His Kingdom first, He will add to your life more than you can ever imagine." Robinson said his goodbyes to Joe, Sue, and Stacy and slipped out the door to continue down the path the Lord had called him to so many years ago.

Frank did not know what the future would hold. He knew he wanted Jesus to be the in the center of his life. He thought about college, football, and maybe becoming a youth pastor, possibly keeping the garage open. The future now held promise, and he wanted Stacy to be a part of it for sure.

The next morning Frank watched as his dad walked into room and gingerly sat on the bedside chair. An awkward silence stretched between them as his father's gazed remained steadily upon him. *So much needed to be said, but where to begin?* "Dad, do you think maybe you could help me take a walk?" Frank asked. After much effort and IV pole wrangling, Frank was able to stand by the bed and hold the rail until he felt relatively steady. Joe offered his shoulder and placed a firm hand on his son's lower back as the two large men inched down the hospital's sterile halls. Neither said a word as Frank took small steps, and Joe matched his pace giving the needed support. It was Frank that stopped and asked directions at the nurses' station for the way to the hospital's chapel.

Once inside Frank and Joe sat in one of the pews soaking up the peaceful silence. Tears welled in Frank's eyes as all the pent-up emotions and regrets began to wash over him in waves. Joe's arm came around him as he reached into his pocket, pulling out a hand-kerchief that they would both probably wind up sharing. "When I left home like I did, I know I hurt you and Mom. I was so hard-headed and angry at God for allowing Mr. Stone to die. You kept loving me, and I rejected everything you taught me to respect. I am so sorry! I love you, and I realize how much you love me. I want to live my life the right way!"

Heavenly Warriors were swinging gleaming swords of holy fire with laser-like precision weakening the enemy's crumbling defenses.

"I know you and Mom and a lot of other people have been praying for me and that God kept me alive for a reason. Dad, in this place before you, I'm rededicating my life to Jesus!"

Light flooded into the small chapel as the final strongholds of darkness were severed and the enemy's power was crushed. All of Heaven rejoiced with the warriors as the prodigal son made his way back toward his Father's care. The path was now clear for true healing to take place.

Silent tears fell as Joe hugged Frank and continued to listen as his son poured out all that God had brought him through. A silent prayer of gratitude helped comfort Joe's breaking heart as he realized his son was being restored to him and his heavenly Father.

"Dad, I would like to come home and live under your roof " Frank paused slightly for humorous effect, "and under your rules!"

"Yes, son! Absolutely!" Joe answered. He recognized that Frank did not need a lecture just an affirming father.

"We better head back to the room. Mom and Stacy might think I ran off again and took you with me!" Frank commented as the pair made the slow journey back to the room. The Savior was at work and the burden of sin had been removed.

Sue and Stacy were sitting in the room, sipping on sodas and eating chips from the hospital's vending machine when Frank and Joe returned. "The nurses at the nurses' station told us where you had gone, but we thought we were going to have to send out a search party after you two," Sue said, as the two men entered the room with enormous smiles on their faces.

With a little effort, they were able to get Frank back into bed. The physical and emotional exhaustion was clear on his face. They talked quietly as Frank's eyes began to droop. They prayed together, said their goodnights, and left the room.

Frank settled in for one of the most peaceful night's rest he had experienced in longer than he could remember. The hourly nurse's check had not even disturbed his tranquility.

In the rental car on the way back to the hotel, Joe shared a small portion of the conversation in the chapel. Stacy listened silently from the backseat as Joe talked. Her heart was still dealing with the ache from the past hurt and shame. *Lord, heal my broken heart!*

Help me to trust You first and to be able to trust Frank not to hurt me!

Over the next few days, Frank's strength and balance returned, and he was able to walk unassisted. They began to make plans to fly back to Iowa and to ship the Harley back to the farm after he was discharged.

Back in Iowa, life was slowly returning to a new normal as Frank reconnected with the church.

* * *

It was a week after getting home that Stacy could have sworn she heard a little voice that said, "Go check on Frank!" She left her house, jumped into the car, and headed toward the familiar Walton-style home. She had always loved that house. She turned down the long gravel drive and saw Frank sitting in one of the rocking chairs on the front porch. "Okay, Lord, is this a mistake?" she half-heartedly prayed, doubting her decision.

Frank stood up slowly when he saw Stacy's car turn in to the driveway. "Lord, guide my words," he said, barely above a whisper, as she got out of the car. "Hey!" Frank called out from the porch steps. "I was about to get me something to drink. You want to join me?" Frank's arm made a sweeping motion to the other rocker on the porch. He then noticed his mom was placing two glasses of lemonade on the small table between the chairs and then disappeared back into the house. *How did she do that?* Frank shook his head when he saw the glasses. Stacy walked up the steps, smiled tentatively at Frank and took a seat. They both knew they were long overdue for a heart-to-heart talk.

He let the quiet of the day settle over them before he began to speak. Slowly he turned his head, locking eyes with Stacy. The tears pooled in Frank's eyes as he began to right the horrible wrong that still lay between them. "Stacy, I am truly sorry. I remember that night I know I hurt you badly and made you not trust me! I want you to know the Lord has changed me!" Frank poured out everything that had occurred from the time of the accident to waking up in the hospital. He shared how he had come face to face with the demons trying to destroy him. He bared his soul telling her things he had not even told Joe. He told her about how real his visions had been the night of the accident. He did not care if she thought he was crazy. He did not want any secrets left between them.

"I know this is a lot to take in, but I love you. I am not the same person who left from here, and I'm going to prove that to you that I have changed. I will work hard to regain your trust. You are worth whatever I have to do. Can we get past this together?

Stacy reached over and grabbed Frank's hand in between both of hers and looked deep into his eyes. She took a deep breath and began, " Frank, I have loved you for as long as I can remember!" The tears began to stream down her cheeks. *Why was this so difficult? She had played out this conversation in her head dozens of times.* "I worried about you constantly for the months you were gone! A part of me never wanted to see you again and another part wanted to hold you tight and know you were okay." The past few days had given her time to examine her true feelings. "Franklin Joseph Carter, I do want to move past this together, but we have to have some rules in place." Stacy could tell by the confused look that she needed to elaborate. "First, we need accountability. If we go out anywhere, it is only with a group or other couples. Second, I would like us to go to counseling with Pastor Steve once a week. You need to call the church office and set that up. Third, I need time; I need us to move slowly. Trust between us needs to be rebuilt so our physical relationship needs to be limited to handholding for a while with no pressure." Frank's relief knew no bounds as he had been imagining the worst. Stacy was right and he agreed, inside he was actually relieved. Thank God she didn't say that she never wanted to see him again.

Valentine's Day was coming up soon, and Frank had been working hard to live a transparent life before his parents, Stacey, his pastor, and the church. He had decided to get his mechanic certification and reopen Mr. Stone's shop, knowing he had a talent with cars that could help him provide for a family. After much prayer and the blessing of his parents and pastor, he approached Mr. McInnis, Stacy's dad, and asked for his daughter's hand in marriage. Thankfully, he said yes with his blessings!

Frank knew that he had to make the proposal special and enlisted the help of Pastor Steve during the church's Valentine's Day service. "Frank, Stacy, could you two help me as we honor a few special Valentines?" They passed out roses to the longest married, the most recently married, and the couple with the most children. Pastor Steve continued, "We have one more couple we would like to honor." Pastor Steve handed the mic to Frank and went and sat next to his wife on the front row.

Frank cleared his throat, "Stacy, going forward, I want to live my life serving Jesus with you by my side!" He knelt and produced Grandma Betty's small engagement ring. "Will you marry me?"

It has been said many times that the eyes are the window to the soul. At that moment, Stacy saw past eyes filled with love and compassion into the soul of a man that had been washed clean by the blood of Jesus. She slowly nodded, "Yes!" They both knew the path might be unknown, but the rest of their journey would be together to the same *final destination!*

Epilogue

eanwhile, as Frank lay recovering in a hospital bed hundreds of miles away, a fifteen-year-old Buick sat parked in front of an old bikers' shop in Denver, Colorado. The miraculous journey of a redhead named Veronica was ongoing. Getting her out of the car was a victory for the warring angels of the Lord that were encamped about Veronica. She walked slowly toward the front door. Despite the attack on all sides by nerves and a fear of the unknown, she worked up the courage to knock. Before she could run away, the door opened, and she was greeted by a small woman and perhaps the largest man she had ever seen. Each wore a warm smile of welcome. "Can we help you?' the enormous man asked.

"My name is Veronica. Tank sent me," her voice squeaked with nervousness.

The small woman smiled and spoke soothingly, "Please come in! Dinner is ready. My name is Victoria, and this is my husband, Tiny."

About the Author

Tim and his wife of over thirty years are lifetime residents of south Louisiana. They have raised two children and are now enjoying being grandparents. Tim has been involved in children's ministry for many years and is delighted when kids meet Jesus. In his free time, Tim enjoys crawfish boils with family and friends, LSU sports, and attending car shows.

Made in the USA
Coppell, TX
30 September 2023